THE CAPTAIN

Griffin Force #2

JULIE COULTER BELLON

STONE HALL BOOKS

THE CAPTAIN

OTHER BOOKS BY JULIE COULTER BELLON

The Capture

Second Look

Lincoln Love Stories

Love's Broken Road

Love's Journey Home

Veterans Club Regencies

The Marquess Meets His Match

The Viscount's Vow

The Highlander's Hidden Heart

Copyright 2016 by Julie Coulter Bellon.

Published by Stone Hall Books

ISBN: 9780692703120

Cover Design by Steven Novak Illustrations

Copyright 2016

Printed in the United States of America

First Printing May 2016

10 9 8 7 6 5 4 3 2 1

ACKNOWLEDGMENTS

Thanks to my Fab Four—Jon Spell, Robyn Wood, Dawn Allen, and Faelynn Butler. You guys are the best at catching my mistakes and making me look good. I am so lucky to have friends like you!

A huge thanks to my critique partner Annette Lyon. It's been so fun getting to know you better. You were a huge motivation to me and made The Captain shine!

Thank you to my SWAT team who are the best street team around! You guys are like my writing tribe and I appreciate you.

And last, but never least, my biggest thanks and all my love goes to my family. They're my biggest cheerleaders who pick up the slack and give me so much support in reaching for my dreams. I love you.

For Nathan who has always loved his Canadian heritage as much as I do.

CHAPTER ONE

Captain Colt Mitchell pressed his back against a low mud brick wall baked hard after years of relentless summer days in Afghanistan. As he crouched in the darkness, he could still feel a bit of warmth coming from the bricks, as if they didn't want to release their heat, even at night. The sun would be up soon, though, and the bricks would be fired in the scorching temperatures all over again.

Leaning forward a bit, he made sure to blend into the shadows, his black tactical gear and camo face paint like a second skin to him now. With one more look at the non-descript two-story house they'd been watching for the past forty-eight hours, he silently let out a breath. They had credible intel that Nazer al-Raimi was using this house as a hideout tonight. This was the first whisper they'd heard on the whereabouts of the AQIM terrorist leader in three months, so they'd jumped on it. And while Colt had wanted this man put away before, the attack on the Parliament buildings in Ottawa made the hunt for Nazer personal for him. The sooner he was in custody the better, even if they had to come to the outer reaches of Afghanistan to do it.

Colt pulled back the Velcro strap covering the illuminated face on his military-issued watch. 0200 hours. Nazer's guards had changed shifts at midnight and they'd switch again any minute. That's when they'd make their move.

"Check in." Commander Jake Williams' voice came over Colt's comms and he quietly tapped his throat mic twice to signal he was in position.

Jake was intense and thorough, both things that made him a good team leader. It had been interesting to see how his Navy SEAL training was similar to Colt's JTF2 training. Apparently Canada and the U.S. had very similar practices for their elite teams. In their search for Nazer these past months, though, Jake's ability to root out details and make educated guesses had gotten them closer to Nazer than they'd ever been before. If all went well, tonight was the night they'd have him in custody. They had two minutes to get in, grab Nazer, and get out. The extraction site was in the foothills just outside of town and Colt was ready to get this done, especially if it ended with Nazer on a helo headed to whatever black ops site waited for him.

Colt took another peek over the wall. Even though it was two a.m., lights blazed from the front windows and five heat signatures still patrolled the house. Pulling back, he heard Jake's voice in his comms. "Incoming."

Colt pulled his tactical face mask down and got his night vision monocular in position. An SUV rumbled up the road and turned down the driveway toward the house. This was it. He watched as four men exited the vehicle. "I have a visual on our target." His pulse picked up. The second man was definitely Nazer.

Their leader's arrival caused some excitement in the house. More lights went on, and agitated voices carried through the night air toward them. "Hold your positions," Jake said quietly.

His voice sounded strained and Colt could relate. They all wanted this to work. Nazer had hurt so many people, caused so much damage and heartache. All for what? A position in the ISIS leadership? Acting out some sort of vendetta on Westerners?

Nazer's latest attack in Ottawa had killed one of Colt's closest friends from his time with Joint Task Force 2, the Special Ops team in Canada. David Reeves had been one of the bravest men he knew. They'd served together in some of the most dangerous countries in the world, but when David was ready to settle down, he took the offer to be on the security detail for the Prime Minister. Not two weeks later he'd been killed at the attack on the Parliament buildings and all the evidence pointed to Nazer being the mastermind behind it. Canada's sense of security was shaken, his friend dead. Colt's hand clenched around his semi-automatic. He needed Nazer to pay and he wanted to be the one to capture him.

The more he thought about what was at stake, the angrier he became and that wouldn't help on this op. He used his tactical breathing—slow breath in, hold for four, then counting to four as he let the breath out. After a few times, Colt was focused.

Ready.

The Griffin Task Force had carefully plotted out this op, and he needed to be calm and in control. No emotion. That was one thing he'd learned being part of JTF2. Execution was easier when your prep, training, and self-control backed you up. Of course he still felt a healthy surge of adrenaline on any op, but that was easily channeled into getting the job done.

A bead of sweat rolled down his back and he adjusted his position a little further away from the brick wall. Not even the warm breeze rolling in every now and then offered any relief from the suffocating heat. Colt rolled his shoulders to shake it off. For just a second he let himself imagine breathing in the chill air of an ice rink and lacing up his skates for a game. That was one thing he missed about his home country and was high on his to-do list when Nazer was taken care of and Colt was back home.

He brought his attention back to the task at hand. Two men were coming out of the front door, and Colt focused on the scene through his night vision monocular. Squinting, he leaned forward. It looked like they were carrying several laptops.

"You s-s-smell that?" Elliott's stutter came over the comms, a bit more pronounced under stress. Colt sniffed the air. He did smell something. Smoke.

"They're cutting and running," Jake said in Colt's ear. Colt turned to look at his team leader, waiting for that go signal. Jake's hand cut through the air. "We're moving in. Go."

Colt pushed forward, staying to the left side of the perimeter. His job was to secure the back entry with Nate Hughes, his partner on this op. They were about six feet apart, both moving through the shadows, making sure they didn't call attention to themselves. Smoke was starting to billow out of the house now and it covered their position even more. Their window of time to grab Nazer had always been short, but with the house on fire, they had about as long as it would take to grab his favorite donut at the Tim Horton's drive-thru. Which wasn't long.

Just before they reached the rear entry, a window on the second floor shattered, and a chair landed with a thud on the ground near Colt. He raised his rifle to the ready, and looked up to see a woman leaning out, screaming, "Help me! Help me!" before being yanked back inside.

"I've got a woman screaming for help on the back side," Colt said into his comms. No one had guessed from the heat signatures that they had a woman in the house. Where had she come from?

"Could be a trap. Stay on target," Jake's voice was firm. "We've got to get in and get out. Move inside on my count."

Colt bit the inside of his cheek. He knew Jake's order was best for the mission, but that woman's scream was desperate and this house was going up in flames. Maybe once they had Nazer wrapped up, he could go after her.

"Three, two, one. Move!"

Colt and Nate moved in through the back door, and gunfire met them immediately. Colt kept low, which also made it easier to breathe with all the smoke coming from the front of the house. From a quick glance, it looked like they'd made a bonfire with furniture in the living room. Jake and Elliott were pinned down and under fire so Colt and Nate quickly shifted from room to room, looking to spot Nazer.

"Not on the main," Colt said into his comms. "Heading upstairs."

With Nate covering him, Colt led the way up the stairs. The crackle of the hungry fire was moving toward them, as if they were what it wanted to devour next.

They needed to hurry.

The hallways were clear, but there were four closed doors. Colt started with the first, staying high while Nate stayed low. They opened the first door. Empty. Before they could go any further, a scream pierced the air. It came from the room at the end of the hall. With a nod to Nate, he headed that way. The door was locked, so Colt raised his leg and focused all his adrenaline to kick it open. The woman was being held, a gun to her head, and Nazer behind her.

"One step closer and the woman will die." The smoke was obscuring Nazer's face and the floor underneath them was starting to groan. Time was nearly out.

"Don't let me die," the woman sobbed in broken Pashto. "Please." Her eyes darted between Colt and Nate as she pleaded between coughs.

"Let her go," Colt ordered. "You're coming with me." He tried to catch Nate's eye. Did he have a shot? Could they risk taking Nazer down with a hostage in front of him?

"Not interested in a deal?" Nazer crouched a little lower and looked out the window.

"No deal." Colt inched forward.

"I'll trade *her* for *you*." Nazer smiled, an evil little smirk that made Colt want to punch it off his face. "I'd prefer Commander Williams, since we have unfinished business, but you'll do."

I'll bet. Jake had been a thorn in Nazer's side for too long and it was practically a vendetta for Nazer now, but there was no way he would get near him. Not if Colt had anything to say about it. "Just give us the woman and come quietly. I promise not to kill you." Colt kept his gun trained on Nazer. If the woman would just move a smidgen to the left he'd have a shot.

"Don't bargain with him, Colt. Get out of there. Retreat. Now." Jake's voice over comms was commanding, nearly angry, but Colt didn't take his eyes off Nazer. Not now. Not when they were this close.

"Do you really think I'd be so foolish not to be prepared for your pitiful attempt to capture me?" Nazer moved slightly, making sure his victim was shielding him. He pressed his gun to her temple, his eyebrow raised as if he expected Colt to answer. The air in the room was being sucked out by the fire and the smoke swirled around their feet. When the floor underneath them started to hiss like a warning, Colt took a step forward. They didn't have time for bargaining. This fire was coming for them.

"We're on our way," Colt heard Jake say, but it was too late. If the fire didn't get them all, Nazer had the advantage in this standoff. If only the woman weren't between them.

The floor groaned again and Nazer straightened. As if realizing they were out of time, he raised his gun. In that split second, Colt saw an opportunity to at least wing the guy, and he pulled the trigger.

A scream rent the air as the woman twisted out of Nazer's grasp and fell on the floor. She scrambled to the window and Colt felt a moment of relief that he hadn't hit her. He rolled toward the door, finding a bit of cover behind a table, but not enough. A shaft of pain went through his arm. More gunshots popped through the air and he heard Nate's cry of pain echoing through his ears. "Nate!"

His partner was on the floor holding his leg. Blood was everywhere. "I'm okay, Captain. Let's get out of here."

The woman was crawling around the perimeter of the

room, trying to get away from the window and Colt could see why. There was a man silhouetted in the window frame motioning for Nazer. *They must have a ladder to the ground floor.* "Nate, can you get her out of here?" he yelled to his partner.

Nate shook his head and yelled back, "No way! I'm not leaving you."

Gunfire erupted again, both Nazer and the man at the window shooting at them like fish in a barrel. Colt returned fire. "That's an order. Now! This whole floor is about to collapse. Get her out!" With his position, there was no way he could make it to the door on the opposite side of the room.

"I'll cover you," Nate said as the woman reached him. He pulled her to his side. "Come on!"

"I'll be right behind you." But Colt knew he wouldn't. He was going to die in this room, but not before he took Nazer with him.

The moment Nate and the woman were through the door, Colt rubbed his bloody arm on his cargo pants to make sure he had a grip, then popped up from his cover position and opened fire. His arm was going numb and his shots were off, but it gave him some satisfaction when Nazer had to duck. He was starting to lose consciousness, his lungs burning from the heavy smoke, but he had enough juice to make one more shot.

This was it.

At the last second, Nazer did a bob and weave and Colt ended up shooting the guy at the window. With a grunt of satisfaction that he'd at least gotten one of them, he let his gun fall to the floor, his body following. The edges of his vision were going dark and he embraced it now. At least he'd provided enough distraction that Nate and the woman could get away. His death wouldn't be for nothing.

He looked up, a little jolt going through him as he realized Nazer was standing above him. Colt lifted his chin. "Go ahead. Finish it."

"Oh, I have plans for you." Nazer hunched over him on the floor, his face inches from Colt's. "And I think I'm going to enjoy this."

CHAPTER TWO

Brenna stoked the fire in the small wood stove, throwing the ends of her hijab back over her shoulder, out of the way. Electricity was spotty in this area of Afghanistan, so Aedala, the house cook, kept the cook fire burning in case they had to use it. Brenna hated adding the heat to an already boiling house. There was no air conditioning, no breeze of any kind from the open kitchen windows, just hot suppressive heat. And as if that weren't enough, Saabir Mattar demanded that all the women in his household wear a burka and hijab, which made the air that much more stifling. Thankfully he didn't require a face covering, but even with that concession, his philosophy toward women was definitely more of a "seen and not heard" sort of thing.

She closed the tiny door on the stove and set the fire poker in the corner. Aedala liked her kitchen orderly and Brenna had learned quickly to do exactly as she was asked. There was a wooden spoon in the corner and Aedala had used it often when

Brenna was new to give her a *thwack* with it if she forgot something. Her knuckles still smarted with the memory of it sometimes.

But Brenna was lucky to be here at all. Inserted into Nazer al-Raimi's first lieutenant's household as an undercover house slave was a small victory. Her nerves had been on edge the entire time Saabir had negotiated to buy her. New to deep cover work, she couldn't control the questions rushing through her mind as she stood there quietly so they could discuss how much she was worth. What if Saabir didn't believe she was from a small country village in the mountains of Afghanistan? She had looks that would pass as an Afghan woman, but there was still a chance that he might not accept the cover story. What if she couldn't handle what she'd be asked to do as a slave? Was he asking so many questions about her background because he was suspicious?

Even with her training and experience in Canadian intelligence behind her, she'd broken the first rule by letting herself lose focus and not paying attention to the details. Saabir had given her a powerful reminder of what could happen when she let her guard down for even a moment, though. He'd stood in front of her and she'd met his eyes, trying to calm her fluttering nerves. He'd slapped her face. Hard.

"Eyes on the floor," he'd yelled in Pashto.

Her cheeks still burned when she thought of how she'd failed the first test of undercover work that day. It was the last time she'd let anything like that happen. With that last forceful bit of instruction, he'd agreed to take her as his new slave, nearly throwing her purchase price at their guy. She'd done her job from that moment forward, always the subservient kitchen worker with her eyes on the floor. The rules actually made it easier to fulfill her mission objectives. Saabir regularly met with his soldiers while dining and discussed AQIM training camp locations and plans for recruitment. He didn't seem to care that a servant girl was almost always in attendance serving them food. She'd gotten all the information she'd overheard to her handler and it had made a ripple in taking down Nazer's part in the war on terror. Brenna was proud of that.

But it wasn't enough.

After AQIM's attack on the Parliament buildings in Ottawa she'd felt a drive to get more information, find more evidence, make sure she was ready to act on even the tiniest clue of what Nazer and Saabir were planning next. There would be another meeting tonight and she was hopeful they might discuss more specifics. The sooner they knew their plans, the sooner they could stop it.

"I'm retiring now," Aedala said to her in Pashto. It was the one language that had taken Brenna months to learn, but had been crucial to making her cover believable. "Make sure the master's food is set out the moment you hear him come in."

Brenna bowed slightly. "I will."

Aedala slowly shuffled out of the kitchen toward the servants' quarters and Brenna let out a long breath. Aedala watched her like a hawk when they were together and it was daunting sometimes. Maybe with a little bit of time to herself, she could sneak into Saabir's office and poke around a little.

But before that thought could really take shape she heard the creak of the heavy metal gates at the front of the house. Someone was coming, most likely Saabir. She grabbed the bowl of *korma* stew, Saabir's favorite, with a plate of *naan* and *chalau* rice, before she headed toward the dining room. If his dinner wasn't waiting for him when he got to the table, she would be the one to feel his wrath. He'd thrown the bowl in her face before and had no problem slapping her as a reminder of the rules. She wasn't eager to have either happen again.

She glanced down the hall before she entered the dining room and was surprised to see Nazer al-Raimi himself standing in the doorway. His swarthy appearance and normal frown had been replaced by a look of victory. Saabir had an arm around an unconscious man who didn't look good at all, blood dripping from a cut on his head. Whoever that guy was, Nazer looked happy to have him in custody. She ducked into the dining room before Saabir or Nazer saw her. It wouldn't be helpful if they caught her staring. She'd find out who the prisoner was soon enough.

She took the food into the dining room and laid it all out exactly as Saabir liked it. Main dish at the top of his plate, bread at the left side, rice at the right. Turning, she swiftly grabbed the napkins and silverware out of the cabinet in the corner of the room and placed those items around the plate. It was perfect. The aroma of the spices from the food wafted to her and she allowed herself a moment of pride. The stew was some of her best work since learning to make it. She'd get her own bowl once Saabir had his fill, but she knew it would taste good. It smelled good. He'd appreciate that.

After taking one last look to make sure everything was as it should be, she pivoted to go back to the kitchen and jumped when she saw Nazer standing in the doorway.

"Your services are needed," he growled at her. She stared at him, a shiver of fear passing through her at the coldness in his black eyes, before she dropped her gaze to the floor. While Saabir would slap her for looking him in the face, Nazer would do worse and enjoy it. He loved inflicting pain.

"*Hao, saaqhib*," she said, automatically. Her heart pounded as she waited with her head down. What was he doing? Staring at the top of her head? *Just keep your eyes down*, she told herself. He was probably testing her or something.

Nazer didn't move or speak and neither did she. Was this to be a strange game of chicken then? Who would blink first? She pulled her hands inside her burka, all her senses attuned to the man in front of her.

"Bring a tray and a jug of water out back," he finally commanded. When she was sure his back was turned, she glanced up in time to see him leave. The man had an air of evilness around him that she couldn't explain, she just felt it in his presence. His instructions echoed through her brain and she suppressed an inward groan. "Out back" was the polite way of saying the torture room they had set up for questioning whatever prisoners they captured. Most of them didn't walk out of it. She wished with all her soul she could save the men who were taken "out back," but she couldn't risk her job. Gathering information on Nazer's operation was imperative, especially since he was gaining the notice of ISIS and becoming so powerful in AQIM. He was a man walking a fine line between two terrorist organizations and that gave him a unique power. If they didn't stop him now, he could grow to be another bin Laden.

No one that she knew wanted that.

She started toward the kitchen a feeling of dread unfurling in her gut. Squashing it, she filled the jug with water and got a tray of *naan* ready. Even though she would only be delivering the food, she would see part of the suffering they were inflicting on their prisoner. She'd watched it too many times already and her nightmares were filled with the images. Locking those feelings away during her waking hours made it possible for her to stay, but in her dreams, she always broke the prisoner out and got him to freedom.

When the tray and jug were ready, she opened the back door that led to the courtyard. The outbuilding they'd taken the prisoner to was located in the far corner, little more than a mud shack. The light was on and she could see shadows moving behind the nearly sheer curtains. The first time she'd seen the inside of the shack, the curtains had stood out to her. Why have any window coverings at all, never mind pretty ones, in a room that was made for torture and the ugliness a man could inflict on fellow human beings? It didn't make sense, but then again, not a lot made sense in the shadow war on terror they were fighting.

As she neared the shack, she heard a crash and stopped momentarily. The questioning was already underway. Her stomach twisted. She didn't want to go in. The helpless feeling completely enveloped her. Her lungs locked and she couldn't get oxygen.

Breathe, she told herself sternly. *Remember why you're here.* She steeled herself for what she was about to see inside that room. With the tray on her hip, she nearly raised her hand to knock before remembering to just do a finger tap. Seen and not heard. That was the mantra for women here.

"*Dakhelawal.*" Nazer sounded annoyed, so she quickly did as he asked and entered the room.

She averted her eyes, but not before she saw a large man thrashing on the bed. He was tall, at least six foot three, and was dressed in black cargo pants and a black t-shirt. He also smelled like a fire pit. She set the tray down on a small table in the corner, trying to glean a few more details, but Saabir was blocking her view. From the sounds of things, though, she could definitely say that the prisoner didn't like being tied down and was doing his best to make sure they knew it.

"Give it to him," Nazer ordered Saabir, who moved to stand near the head of the bed. Saabir dwarfed Nazer in size, but there was no doubt as to who was in charge.

She watched as Saabir took out a needle and jabbed it into the prisoner's arm. His one eye that wasn't black and swollen glared daggers at Nazer and Saabir, and his fists clenched around the ropes that held him down. The gag prevented the prisoner from fully voicing his displeasure, but while the words were nearly unrecognizable, their meaning was clear. And if she wasn't mistaken, those were English curses he was spewing at them. Was he American? Canadian? Where had he been caught?

She had no answers to her questions, and neither would Nazer until whatever they'd given him wore off. Within moments, the thrashing stopped and he was still. Brenna quickly turned her attention back to the food, not wanting to have her interest in the prisoner noted by either Nazer or Saabir.

"We'll question him further in the morning," Nazer said in Pashto. "We need more light for the pictures." He went over to the tray, barely acknowledging her as he took a bite of the *naan* and poured himself a glass of water. "We'll see what we can get out of him before we dangle him as bait for Commander Williams."

Brenna kept her eyes on the floor but made note of the name, storing it away for her next check-in. Whoever Commander Williams was, Nazer was taking a big risk. With an attack on the horizon, he didn't have time to play games like this, but he was doing it anyway. That said something about his importance. Maybe they could track Commander Williams down and use him against Nazer somehow. Her spirits lifted. This could possibly lead to the break she'd been waiting for.

"Is my meal in the dining room?" Saabir asked, chewing on his portion of the *naan* and finally noticing her.

She nodded once.

"All of the courses are ready?"

She nodded again, knowing Saabir didn't expect a response beyond that. It wasn't like she could say no to him.

"Clean up in here, then come serve the meal in the house." He brushed by her as if she weren't there and left the room with Nazer behind him. Now it was just Brenna and the unconscious prisoner. She went to the window and parted the pretty curtains. Nazer and Saabir were halfway back to the house. Letting the curtains fall again, she glanced at the prisoner. She couldn't get too attached, didn't want to know anything about him that would add to the nightmares she already suffered, but there was something about him.

She went to the side of the metal cot and looked down at his face. Her heart rate sped up and she blinked, not believing what her eyes were seeing. The nose that was just a little crooked, the proud chin, the short dark hair. A roar of blood rushed through her ears and she grabbed the side table for support. She knew this man. Once upon a time, she'd known his face almost as well as her own.

How can Colt Mitchell be here? When she left to join counter-intelligence and he joined Joint Task Force 2, she'd thought she'd never see him again. Why was he here? She immediately reached for the bonds strapping him to the bed before she pushed her instinct down. She couldn't untie him. She couldn't help him at all.

Clenching her fists, she tried to quell the panic rising within her. Colt would recognize her and her cover would be blown. Not to mention that Nazer would kill them both. She had to get him out. But helping him in any way would blow her cover as well. She was stuck.

What could she do?

Taking a breath and letting it out, she brushed his hair back. His cheek was swelling, the eye above it already swollen shut, and he was covered in soot. He'd obviously been in a fire and a fight. Turning him slightly she could see an angry burn on his neck. At least that was one thing she could help him with. Quickly grabbing the discarded cloth napkin from the side table, she dipped it in the water jug. She glanced back at the unconscious man, still trying to wrap her brain around the fact that Colt was here. She wrung out the napkin and came back to his side, gently pressing the wet fabric against the burn. It wouldn't do much, but at least it was something.

Standing there, offering such a small comfort, she felt tears clog her throat. Once he was awake her hands would be tied, and she wouldn't be able to even offer him water. Could she really watch him suffer?

Biting her lip, she dipped the napkin in the cool water once more. So many memories of their time together, the flirting, the fun, the way he'd looked at her when they'd said goodbye. How could they have come to this?

"I'm sorry," she whispered as she drew back and picked up the tray. Closing her eyes for a moment, she gathered herself, then left the room and shut the door.

CHAPTER THREE

Colt opened his eyes to a weak pool of light filtering in through the dirty window. His head pounded at the sight of it. He closed his eyes again and lay back on the foul-smelling cot to try and piece together exactly where he was. Exhaustion pressed down on him, and he couldn't shake the grogginess. All that seemed to be registering right now was how much his body hurt, his shoulder, neck, and head being the worst. He'd received a few injuries during his military service, but the only other time he'd felt like this was when he'd taken a hard check during a hockey game and ended up flat on his back on the ice with a concussion.

Determined to get his bearings, he tried to gently turn his head, but that was difficult since he could only see out of one eye. What was the best way to look around that would cause him the least amount of pain? He decided to do it in small increments, moving his head a little more every time he breathed in. The pain was more bearable that way.

From the looks of things he was alone in a tiny hovel, no bigger than his bedroom back home. The only furniture was the metal cot he was on, and a small wooden table and chair in the corner. He tried to move his hands, but realized that part of the pain in his shoulder was the fact that his arms were wrenched upwards and tied to a stake above the bed. With the cobwebs beginning to clear from his mind, he took a mental inventory, moving his legs, feet, and torso. Nothing seemed broken, but he hurt all over.

He lay back, still trying to piece together exactly what happened after Nazer had shoved him through the window. The blow to the back of his head. The feeling of being dragged away. Put in a truck and bounced for hours over bumpy roads. He hadn't been conscious for some of it. He remembered needles in his arm, the look in a man's eyes as he'd drugged Colt. It was starting to come back. He closed his eyes, wanting to give in to the darkness and go back to sleep, but knowing he had to stay as alert as possible.

What are they shooting me up with? Whatever it was had a killer hangover. He couldn't remember ever feeling this wasted and out of it. *Get yourself together.*

With a tiny shake of his head to emphasize that thought, he made a mental to-do list. The first thing on the agenda was getting out of his bindings. The gag was pretty loose, and he was able to work it off his mouth without too much trouble. Check that one off. He licked his cracked lips and, for just a moment, forgot about his pain when his thirst kicked itself up to the front of the line. His mouth was drier than the Registan desert in July. What he wouldn't give for a swallow of water. Colt grimaced, knowing that was probably the least of his worries. But his body was starting to wake up a little more from the drugs and that was a good thing.

With his success at getting the gag off, Colt started working on the knots that held his wrists to the stake. There was a slim chance he could escape, but he'd have to do it before Nazer came back. There was no telling what shape Colt would be in after Nazer was through with him. Best to get out now, while he had a chance, before any torture started. When Nazer had promised to enjoy what he had planned for Colt, there was no doubt he meant it.

His mind raced back to Jake and the team. Were they looking for him? Had Nate made it out okay or was his bullet wound to the leg more serious? Colt couldn't let himself dwell on that one too much. He was going to need all his mental strength for what was ahead of him.

He was making some progress on the thin rope holding his right wrist, when he heard something outside. He stilled. Muffled footsteps heralded someone approaching the hut. Was it Nazer already?

The door creaked opened slowly and a woman entered. She turned the doorknob as she closed it, obviously trying to minimize any noise she made. She didn't face him for a moment and all Colt could see was the back of her dark blue hijab. From the tension in the set of her shoulders, he could tell she was nervous. Maybe if he could build a rapport of some sort with her, she could be an ally for him. Or at least get him some water.

"*Salam Aleikum,*" he said. He knew that was hello in Pashto, but he really understood more of it than he could speak. Hopefully she knew some English.

She finally turned around, and Colt had to blink his one good eye. Either those drugs were more powerful than he thought, or he was looking at Brenna Wilson's doppelganger. With her hair hidden under the hijab, the face that stared back at him was in stark relief. She had Brenna's same nose that turned up slightly at the end, the high cheekbones and tanned skin. They were features a lot of women had, but not many had eyes like hers. Wide, perceptive, a mixture of burnished gold with green flecks that made the color unique to Brenna. From the day they'd said goodbye, those eyes had haunted his dreams. But there was no way she could be here. She was in Canada, working a desk job for the Canadian Security Intelligence Service. Not in Afghanistan.

The woman approached him slowly, her gaze full of anxiety and sadness. He shifted on the cot. Those drugs were playing with his mind. It was the same look his Brenna had the night she'd told him goodbye and he'd hated it then, like he hated it now. He let out a breath and turned his head, deciding he didn't have to look at her, just talk to her. *If she's really here and not a figment of my imagination,* he thought. Maybe she was a hallucination. But why would he hallucinate Brenna? They'd broken up years ago. "Water?" he asked. When he didn't hear any movement he turned back, blinking just to make sure she was still there.

The woman set down her tray on the side table and poured him a half glass. She brought it over and knelt next to the cot. Putting her hand behind his head, she lifted the glass to his parched lips and he drank it greedily. If he was hallucinating, he didn't want to wake up.

He looked up and their gazes locked. "Thank you."

She nodded and her hijab fell back revealing rich, brown hair. Brenna had had hair like that. He'd loved to run his fingers through it. At the military academy she'd always had it pulled back in a tight bun, so at the end of the day it had been their little ritual for him to take it down. He still dreamed about that sometimes, the smile on her face, the silky feel of her hair. Colt stared at the woman in front of him, fighting to wrap his brain around what was happening, but those drugs wouldn't release their hold.

The woman didn't drop her gaze, her brows furrowing as she spoke. "I only have a moment before Nazer gets here. You can't act like you know me or recognize me at all. I'm here undercover, Colt, and I need to stay in place."

"Bren?" She was here. Brenna was in Afghanistan. "Is this some sort of trick?" Maybe those drugs they'd given him were a time release and he'd gotten a second wind of it or something.

She leaned down and put her finger to his lips. So soft, just the lightest brush, but her touch ignited the feelings he'd buried for her long ago. Brenna. He'd never felt a connection like they'd had for any other woman. He'd missed that. If he was going to hallucinate her, well, he was going to enjoy it. He kissed the tip of her finger. "If this is a dream, I don't want to wake up."

She pulled her hand away, her eyes wide and full of surprise. "Colt, you've got to snap out of this. I'm not a dream. You have to listen to me."

Yep. That was the Brenna he knew. Bossy and beautiful. "I don't want to talk anymore. Come a little closer." His mind was sending off warning bells, her words echoing through his muddled brain. What if this wasn't a dream?

She leaned in, but not close enough for him. He stared at her mouth, just out of his reach. "Colt." She tilted his chin upward to meet her eyes. "I know things are confusing right now, but just remember, you don't know me. You can't know me. All right? Remember that."

"I don't know you," he repeated slowly. "Okay." Her desperate tone penetrated the haze of his thoughts and he frowned. If this wasn't a hallucination and she really was here in Afghanistan, she was in a lot of danger.

"Good." Her gaze lingered on him for a moment before she stood. She pulled her hijab back into place before she turned for the door. "I'm going to do what I can to help you. Stay strong," she murmured before she was gone.

The door shut softly behind her and Colt closed his eyes. What were the chances that the girl he'd fallen in love with while they were in Military Intelligence school would turn up on a mission in Afghanistan? In the same place as Nazer al-Raimi? She'd said she was here undercover, but what intelligence agency would be crazy enough to insert a woman into Nazer's network? There was no "intelligence" about that. That sort of mission was so far past dangerous it was in the suicidal zone. A frustrated groan sounded in his throat. She said she'd try to help him and that was the one thing she couldn't do. It would only get both of them killed and he didn't want her sacrificing herself for him.

He wanted to yell, to call her back, to tell her to leave, now. But all he could do was lie there and try to get those drugs out of his system so he could think. *Find something to focus on.* He pulled on his ropes again with renewed energy and ignored the pain as the bonds bit into his wrists. If he could only get one hand free, he might have a chance of getting out of here and taking Brenna with him.

Yet even with his best efforts all he managed to do was make his wrists bleed. The knots wouldn't budge. Lying back, he stared at the ceiling. Nazer was coming any minute now. It would probably be better to focus on remembering his resistance-to-interrogation training. His lungs squeezed at the thought and an icy chill of fear slithered up his spine. Nazer was ruthless. There was no way Colt could prepare for the torture he knew he was facing, but he had to try.

He tried to pull up his memories of that long-ago class of what-to-do-if-you're-captured, his brain still sluggish. How long before that drug wore off? He finally pulled up a memory of Colonel Edwards, a decorated Vietnam War vet, whose voice had reverberated over the class like he was still out in the field commanding his men. He'd ticked off the resistance-to-interrogation steps on his fingers until they'd all memorized them. What were they? Colt frowned, digging deeper into his memory banks. He could see the classroom in his mind, the colonel at the front, barking the information at them. Stay mentally alert. Always exaggerate injuries. Appear weak, but stay strong. Take any chance to eat or drink when it's in front of you. Give a kernel of the truth if you have to, but never the whole truth.

Colt let out a breath of relief, pleased his mind had remembered something clearly. The more time he had to get mentally alert before Nazer's appearance, the better. But, as if fate knew what was happening, Colt heard footsteps outside the hut. Part of him wanted it to be Brenna, so he could get more information about her situation, but at the same time, he wanted her to stay away from him. Nazer would kill them both and think nothing of it.

The door flew open and Nazer entered the room with the large man who'd given Colt the needle last night by his side. "Good morning, Captain Mitchell."

Colt started at the use of his title, but quickly masked his reaction.

Nazer stood over him, his traditional *pakol* hat making him look more like the mug shot everyone on the task force had been looking at the last few months. "You didn't think I knew your name, did you? I know a lot about your pathetic Griffin Force. It's my policy to know everything about my enemies, but it's not you I want." He motioned the man next to him forward. He had a camera and began to take pictures of Colt. He looked away, but Nazer jerked his chin back. "Look into the camera for your friends. I want Julian Bennet and Jake Williams to recognize you."

Colt never had liked his picture taken in the best of circumstances, but this little photo shoot of him tied to a bed, wounded and bleeding, was excruciating. It would be emotionally hard on his team to see the pictures, which was what Nazer wanted. Hatred for the man welled up inside Colt, roiling through his bloodstream. He stared up at the timbers in the ceiling, trying to keep his mind occupied on something other than the clicks of the camera, but the only thing that came to mind was Brenna. Where was she? How was she involved in this? If Nazer had laid one finger on her . . .

His jaw clenched so hard his teeth should have ground into dust. When the clicks stopped, Colt glared at Nazer still standing at the foot of the cot. "What now?" Colt asked, not expecting an answer, but needing to ask.

"I dangle the bait." Nazer came around the cot and leaned down close to Colt's face. "How's the head? I admit, I thought Saabir might have struck you too hard before we loaded you into the truck. You dropped like you were dead."

Colt took a deep breath in, then head-butted Nazer, catching him right in the nose. He cried out and staggered back, blood spurting everywhere. Colt twisted his body and slammed his boot into Nazer's stomach and he fell to the floor. "I'm feeling a lot better now," Colt gasped out. "Thanks for asking."

Saabir was on him in seconds, his ham fists pummeling Colt's mid-section, stealing his breath. The headbutt had cost him, with the pain from the blows racing through his body like hot knives searing him, but seeing Nazer bleeding on the floor was worth it.

"Give him whatever is in that syringe. Now! I don't care if it kills him!" Nazer screamed.

Saabir whipped around and grabbed the syringe. Colt flinched away, not wanting that drug anywhere near him, but the needle pinched his skin and he felt himself slipping away again.

"I'm going to kill you," he promised before the darkness took him completely.

CHAPTER FOUR

The day was dragging. Brenna couldn't keep her eyes off the shack where Colt was being kept. He'd seemed so confused this morning. Saabir's drug cocktail had really done a number on him. He'd remembered her, though. Her fingertips still tingled where he'd kissed her. Whenever she'd imagined them meeting again, it had been in an intelligence briefing or some other professional context. Definitely not in Afghanistan while she was undercover and he was a prisoner. With their backgrounds, though, maybe she should have expected it.

She sat down on the wooden chair in the courtyard, angling it so she could have the shack in her line of vision without it being obvious. Aedala had sent her out to pluck the chickens and it was the first time Brenna had cheerfully done the hated chore. She picked up the first dead bird by the neck and began plucking out the feathers. It was hot, back-breaking work, but she felt better keeping an eye on Colt. Plus, she liked being in the courtyard. It was one of the few places that had any green to it. The small garden near the back door with all its little green plants and shoulder-high trees that offered a little shade were like a little oasis in the sea of Afghanistan brown—brown dirt, brown roads, and brown houses.

She got down to work, but before she'd plucked a two-inch section of feathers to stuff in Aedala's cloth bag, she heard footsteps approaching from the direction of the house. Brenna didn't have to turn around to know it was Saabir. He seemed to be at her elbow from the moment she'd come in from the shack last night until she'd retired to her bed. It unnerved her, but she couldn't let it show so she didn't raise her head, just kept plucking.

"*Mrayray*, you have an assignment."

Brenna kept her breathing even. She hated being called a slave, but that's what she was here. It made her appreciate her freedom at home all the more. "What would you have me do? Aedela has given me extra chores."

And she'd been in a bad mood from the moment they got to the kitchen this morning. Brenna had been careful to do her assigned chores the way Aedala liked them done and she'd kept one eye on the wooden spoon near her arm. The woman was definitely in the mood to find any excuse to give Brenna's knuckles a rap with it. Another reason she'd been happy to escape to the courtyard, even if it meant she had to pluck a chicken.

"You do what I say." Saabir stepped closer and gripped her arm to stop her plucking. She resisted the urge to pull away or wipe some feathers off her hands onto him. He wanted to have a reason to punish her and any movement that could be construed as disobeying him would bring a backhand or worse down on her head. She held very still and kept her eyes on the ground as he brought his face close to hers, his fingers digging into her arms. Her breath caught. Saabir was bolder today. Was that because Nazer was here? He made Aedala's wooden spoon look trivial. "You will sit at the *bandi's* bedside."

Involuntarily her eyes lifted to meet Saabir's. His chin nearly touched his chest, the sunlight glinting off his shaved head. His brows slashed downward as his eyes bored into her, giving him a demonic look. Uneasiness squeezed her chest. He'd never had her stay with the prisoners for any length of time. She'd always just delivered meals and water. Why would he need her to sit with Colt? "Is he ill?" The Pashto language slid off her tongue effortlessly, even though the words wanted to stick in her throat. Had something happened to Colt already?

His jaw tightened. "There was an incident this morning and he's having difficulty with the medication. He's useless now and you will sit there and monitor him until he's lucid, then you will inform me immediately."

Brenna didn't react except for a brief nod, but inside she felt lightheaded with relief. She could watch over him. "What shall I tell Aedela?"

"Just get to your post. I will take care of her." He strode away in the direction of the kitchen, the corners of his knee-length shirt flapping behind him. She had to admit, the traditional menswear of baggy pants and a long loose shirt seemed more practical for the climate than the burka.

When he was inside, Brenna allowed herself a small smile. Brushing stray feathers off her burka, she headed toward the shack. From a practical side, if Colt wasn't aware of what he was saying, she was definitely the best person to sit with him, but a part of her whispered she just wanted to be with him. She wasn't examining that bit of awareness too closely.

Her sandals were quiet on the packed dirt as she hurried down the path. Easing open the heavy wooden door, she slipped inside. The dirty windows made it difficult to get a lot of light into the room, so she pulled the chain on the hanging bulb. Colt was moving restlessly on the metal cot, his arms still tied above his head. If possible, he looked worse than he had last night. His t-shirt was sweaty and plastered to his skin, and the darkening bruises on his face made him look like a down-on-his-luck prizefighter. She bit her lip, feeling helpless in the face of his suffering. What could she do?

His forehead was still crusted with blood from the cut there and she decided that's where she would start. She went to the side table and dipped the bottom edge of her burka in the luke-warm water from the pitcher. After wringing it out, she brought it to Colt's forehead and began to wipe away the blood. Leaning down, she whispered, "Shh, I'm here now."

He stilled and turned in her direction, but didn't open his eyes. "Bren?"

She glanced around, glad she hadn't seen any of Saabir's guards near the shack. Not only because they couldn't hear him call her name, but so they couldn't see the tears gathered in her eyes. He still knew her. No matter what they'd done to him, he recognized her. "I'm going to take care of you."

She was careful as she wiped the blood from the area around his blackened eye. It was so swollen, he probably couldn't see out of it, but his good eye was open and looking at her now. His hands jerked toward her, as if they wanted to reach out, but his wrists were still tied to the bed. She debated untying him, but knew Saabir would punish her if she did. "Just stay still."

"Where am I?"

His voice was raspy so she turned to get him a bit of water. How could she answer him? Had the drugs really made him forget? Or did he want to know his location? She decided to sidestep the question altogether. If he'd forgotten the mess he was in even for a moment, she wouldn't be the one to remind him.

"There was a problem and I was sent in undercover to help you." She hoped that would satisfy him for now. Sure it was only a half-truth, but it was probably better to wait until he was a little more aware before she reminded him of what was going on. His head tilted as he stared at her, obviously trying to make sense of her words. "It's okay. Trust me."

She lifted his head so he could get some water and he drank it greedily. "I'm so thirsty."

Brenna filled the glass and helped him drink again. "You should just rest."

He lay back, his good eye fastened on her. He pulled on the ropes that held him fast to the bed. "Why am I tied to the bed? You and Jack pulling a prank on me?"

Jack Roche had been the third member of their three musketeers group at the military intelligence academy. She'd lost track of him in the last few years, though. "I haven't seen Jack," she said as she leaned closer. "Rest now."

"This is some sort of prank. I know it. Just untie me." His eye had that familiar brown twinkle she'd seen nearly every day she'd been at the academy. "I'll make it worth your while." He gave her a half-smile that still turned her heart over in her chest and he wiggled his hands above his head. How many times had she found comfort and strength in his arms when she'd been stressed out or upset? He had an uncanny way of reading her and knowing exactly what to say to shake off any mood. She'd loved that about him.

But that was then. Everything was different now.

"You're getting cocky, lieutenant. Stand down." She smiled and shook her head. It was so easy to fall into their old patterns, to go back to a time when life was simpler.

"I'm not cocky, I'm confident." He bent his head toward her. "And I'm a captain now."

Well, at least he was starting to remember the present. That was a good sign. "You pulling rank on me?"

"Only if I have to." That half-smile turned into a full-blown grin and the butterflies in her stomach that had been nearly dead from disuse suddenly took flight. How could he still do that to her, all these years later? She stood, needing some space from the feelings he was evoking in her.

"You're leaving me again, aren't you?" he accused, his smile vanishing. His brow furrowed, the same way it had the day they'd said goodbye. "I don't want you to go."

His voice was low, barely above a whisper now and she turned to wet the cloth again. "I'm not going to leave you."

She finished cleaning off the last of the blood on his face and he closed his good eye at her ministrations. Brenna leaned in, needing him to feel her presence, to know she wasn't leaving. She was here and wanted to do what she could to help him. "Where do you hurt the most?" she asked softly.

"My shoulder." He opened his eye again, scrutinizing her face. "My heart when you left me."

Brenna couldn't regain her equilibrium, those words slamming into her well of guilt and regret. It was on the tip of her tongue to say she'd been wrong, she never should have left him, but what good would it do now? She'd broken his heart. There was no coming back from that. "I'm here now."

"I tried not to miss you," he murmured, turning away from her so she had to bend down to catch his words. "But I did. Miss you." His eyes closed and he was slipping back into the drug's hold. Brenna knew sleep was best for him, but she wanted to explain.

"A job in intelligence doesn't make for a great relationship," she whispered near his ear. "You know that. We both knew that." So why was her heart pounding at the thought he'd missed her? Was it because she'd missed him, too?

His body relaxed in slumber, the conversation over for now. A small part of Brenna was glad. She wasn't prepared to rehash her past with him and examine her feelings about seeing him again. It was a surprise he hadn't written her off completely after she'd walked away, but it was obviously still painful.

Her heart squeezed thinking about how much she'd loved him once and how those feelings hadn't died like she thought they would. Even though he was filthy, his clothing torn, his body disoriented from drugs, she pulled her chair close and laid her head on his chest, just over his heart. She'd never thought to see him again and here they were, in Afghanistan, the worst possible place for a reunion. *What am I doing?*

The reassuring *thump, thump,* of his heart under her ear seemed to beat in time with her own. Colt had been her first love, the man she'd entrusted her heart to, even knowing their relationship wouldn't end in a house with a white picket fence. She'd worked her entire life to have a career in intelligence and she couldn't give up that dream—or let him give up his dream of being in Special Ops, either. More than that, a relationship where they were constantly separated would never work. Although, today, looking down at Colt, her decision to break things off with him didn't seem as cut and dried. If she'd known then how difficult the road she'd chosen would be, would she have made a different choice? Maybe.

We can get through this. Her mind echoed the same words Colt had said to her when she'd come to say goodbye five years ago. But she didn't think they could then and it was more than iffy now. Back then she'd felt justified in her decision when both of them were given practically opposite assignments, her with CSIS and him with JTF2. Those assignments certainly hadn't made the separation any easier. She'd thrown herself into her work to forget him, but all those buried feelings were surfacing now. What was she going to do?

Tears stung the back of her throat and she willed them away. *No more pity parties,* she scolded herself. Standing, she tried to carefully turn him over so she could see his shoulder. Maybe she could ease a bit of his pain.

Lifting his torn shirt, she saw a lot of dried blood and an angry red slash going from the back of his neck down his shoulder blade. The cut looked deep, but was only oozing a bit of blood. Certainly having his hands tied above his head wasn't helping anything, though. She took a second to think. If she untied him and Saabir complained she'd just say she was treating his wounds to bring him back around. Would he believe that? It was worth a shot.

She reached up to untie his right hand. She set it on his chest, knowing it would be numb and painful for a while. He didn't move. Kneeling, she reached under the bed and pushed aside Saabir's large case he used for enhanced interrogations. There was nothing in there she wanted. There was a smaller first aid kit behind it and that's what she needed to clean and bandage his shoulder.

Opening up the box, she was glad to see a bottle of antiseptic, cotton balls, and plenty of bandages. She took out the antiseptic and a handful of cotton balls. Crossing to the other side of the bed, she folded his now free arm over his torso and slowly pushed him onto his side. Pulling his shirt up to take his arm out of it proved to be more difficult than she'd thought. There were so many bruises on his body, he flinched with every touch or movement and he began to thrash on the bed. "Shh," she said again. "Let me help you."

After a good look at the wound, she began the painstaking job of cleaning it. "This might sting a bit," she said and winced when he jumped at the first contact with the antiseptic. She worked as quickly as she could and when she was done she'd used every bit of antiseptic the kit had. Quickly taking the butterfly bandages, she did the best she could to put the skin edges back together. He was going to have a massive scar, that was for sure. Looking over his bare chest, it would be joining quite a few other scars. He had a criss-cross of marks across his back, and several other marks decorated his side, some long, some jagged. Colt had definitely seen action in JTF2 and it hadn't been kind to him. Would he change anything if he could go back?

Pulling his t-shirt back down, she wiped a bead of sweat off her forehead. What she wouldn't give for a bit of air conditioning and a day without her burka. She was never going to take lightweight material for granted again. Adjusting her heavier clothing, she pulled the chair next to the bed. Colt seemed more peaceful now and her own anxiety had decreased.

Beyond the bruises and scars, he hadn't changed much since she'd seen him last. His dark brown hair was still military-short. His nose was still a bit crooked from a hockey-puck-to-the-face accident when he was a teen and, combined with his black eye, he looked like a goalie who never wore a face mask. She ran a hand over his jaw, letting her thumb brush over the cleft in his chin. How had he gotten himself into this mess? And how could she help him get out of it?

She wasn't due to report in for another week, but she had to get a message to someone that Colt was here. Maybe her handlers could do something. Alert JTF2 if that's who he was working for. A tiny ray of hope flickered, then died. If she were being realistic, the possibilities were slim. *If* she got word out, *if* they found out who he was working for, *if* they could get here in time, *if* Nazer didn't kill him first. That was a lot of "if." And through it all, she had to keep her cover until they knew where Nazer was going to attack next.

"Hey, there," Colt said, turning his face to her again. His voice was sleepy, as if he was faraway, still semi-dreaming. "Let's go to the Grizzly Grill tonight, eh? Then we can go dancing at Stages after."

Back in the day, whenever they'd had a spare moment to

relax, that was their go-to date. Now, she looked around the dingy shack they were in. What she wouldn't give to be heading to the Grizzly Grill with him tonight. His free hand reached for her and she took it with both of her own.

"I think we need to stay in tonight. You're sick."

He sighed and said, "okay," before he let himself go back to sleep. She sat there, holding his hand, tracing the back of it with her fingers. There was no denying what she had to do. She couldn't put aside her feelings for him and look at this objectively. Not with so much still unsaid between them. She couldn't be the reason he died here.

Getting his whereabouts out to her superiors was a risk to her life and her mission, but she had to take it. She could never live with herself if she didn't.

CHAPTER FIVE

C olt opened his eyes, but one was so swollen he couldn't see out of it very well. His head felt like someone had bashed it in with a hockey stick. He was half-blind and the room was spinning. Closing his eyes, he focused on the room, the light bulb sending daggers of pain straight to his brain. He tried to focus on the shadows to get his bearings. His senses told him he needed to be on alert and as soon as the thought entered his mind, there was a rustle in the corner. He wasn't alone.

Slowly turning his head, he saw Brenna watching him from a chair next to the bed. She'd been such a vivid part of his dreams, for just a second he thought he might still be asleep. He cleared his throat, the thought occurring to him that he might have spoken aloud to her when he wasn't himself. Hopefully he hadn't embarrassed either of them since his feelings for her had been so close to the surface.

"Hey," he said, trying to read the expression on her face. Her lips were pursed tight and she was staring at him. Was she upset? Had he said something?

She blew out a breath. "You're finally awake." Her hand reached out to him, but she pulled it back and folded her arms. "Do you remember your name?"

"Colt Mitchell. What's going on?"

"What's the capital of Canada?"

"Ottawa." He furrowed his brow, trying to recall what he knew about why Brenna was here. "Do you need my rank and serial number next? Are you the newest interrogator or something?"

She frowned. "That's not funny. I'm supposed to let Saabir know when you're lucid so *he* can interrogate you."

Pieces were starting to come back to him now. The raid to grab Nazer. The explosion. He'd been tied to this bed and drugged. No wonder his head was killing him and his dreams had been so real. One wrist was still high above his head, but his right hand was untied. Had she done that? "Are there any video or audio devices in here? Can we speak freely?"

She hunched over and clasped her hands in her lap. "The electricity grid is spotty, so Saabir and Nazer don't have any equipment out here unless they bring it themselves and set up a generator. We're safe."

He breathed a sigh of relief. "Okay, then help me get out of here."

Her mouth flattened and she shook her head. "Do you think I don't want to? The second I do, my mission is compromised, but I can't just leave you here to die, either."

"What mission? Who are you working for?" His gut twisted at the thought of her here on a daily basis, in contact with some of the world's most dangerous men. Who would have put her in that position? But from the look on her face she wasn't going to tell him.

"I could ask you the same questions. How did Nazer capture you? Who are *you* working for?" She stared at him, unblinking. "Is there any way a rescue mission for you might already be underway?"

He hoped so, but the chances were slim. Colt closed his eyes. "I don't even know where I am and Nazer doesn't exactly give out his address to just anyone."

She stood and began to pace, pushing her hijab off her head and rubbing her neck. "I'll take that as a no."

He watched her for a moment, her burka swishing around her feet every time she made another circuit around the room. "I'm with one of the best teams in the world. They're probably looking for me right now, but pacing around isn't going to do either of us any good. Sit. We can figure this out." She'd always liked to pace when she was thinking through a problem, but right now it made him dizzy.

"I'm not under your command, Captain." She came over to the bed and looked down at him, trying to hide her anxiety. If he hadn't known her stress signs, he would have missed them, but she was biting the inside of her cheek and clasping her left wrist with her right hand. Those had been her tells from the day they'd taken their first test at the academy.

She slowly let out a breath as if unsure of what she was about to say. "I have a way to contact my people to let them know you're here and need extraction, but it's dangerous."

He couldn't help staring. She was so different, yet still seemed like the same Brenna he knew. Physically, she hadn't changed much. Even with the burka hiding her curves, her face and the way she carried herself told him she was still fit and had kept up her athletic build. Her hair was pulled back tight against her head, just like it had been at the academy. And her eyes were still filled with the same determination to get the job done. But she had an air of resolve around her now, like she was settled into herself and the life she'd chosen. A very dangerous life. So many conflicting feelings warred within him at that thought.

"Don't put yourself out for me. I can handle whatever Nazer's got." He didn't want Brenna in danger because of him. No matter why they'd ended, she owned part of his heart and always would. He wanted her to stay safe.

She ran her hands over her face and sank back down into the chair. "You don't understand. He enjoys inflicting pain."

"I know a lot more about Nazer than you think. I know what he's capable of."

"Then you know you're going to be tortured." Worry shadowed her eyes.

"I'm a trained soldier." He wished his voice sounded stronger to reassure her. And himself.

"I couldn't bear it." Her voice was soft and she dropped her gaze to her hands folded in her lap. "The things I've seen . . ." She trailed off and his heart sank. Even though they'd both trained for a life like this, in that moment he wished they were normal people back in Canada doing normal things. Not operatives in Afghanistan forced to see the worst of humanity.

"Brenna." He took her hand in his and squeezed. "Maybe *you* need to get out. Go to your handlers and ask for your own extraction."

Her head snapped up. "What?" The warmth that had been between them was sucked away and she yanked her hand back like it had been burned. "I'm not leaving. I've worked too hard to get this far."

He shouldn't have been surprised. She hadn't changed at all. Nothing came before the job, not even good judgment. "The fact that we know each other compromises your mission. It's too dangerous and not worth it. If they find out you're connected to me in any way, they'll kill us both." She had to see that.

She folded her arms and looked back at the door before she turned and spoke. "The attack on the Parliament buildings in Ottawa was just a precursor. We know Nazer's putting a team in place that will use bombs to maximize loss of life, but we don't know where. I'm close to finding out."

Colt clenched his one free fist. That was exactly what he didn't want to hear. "We hit one of Nazer's training camps a week ago and found dozens of barrels of hydrogen peroxide. We think he's making up a new batch of TATP."

Brenna sucked in a breath. "He used TATP in the Ottawa bombing, but three of the bombers blew up before they reached their target. Would he really use it again when it's so unstable?"

Colt shrugged, but that movement was like a knife to his shoulder. He reached up and gingerly touched it. "We confiscated it all, of course, but you know that's not Nazer's only stash." He twisted his neck to get a better look at his shoulder. "Did you bandage me up?"

"I did the best I could. You have a pretty deep cut." She reached over him and pulled his collar down to get a better look. "The bleeding looks like it's stopped anyway."

The edge of her hijab was tickling his forehead as she bent over him and her closeness reminded him of how it had been between them years ago. She'd been at the top of all the classes they'd taken together, and during study groups, she'd combined those smarts with some sass. She'd been irresistible to him. He'd thought the feeling was mutual, but she left without looking back. He tamped down those memories and pulled away a little, trying to put some distance between them. "Thanks for patching me up."

She seemed to sense his discomfort and took a step away. Her eyes narrowed as she looked at him, but he didn't drop his gaze. Let her think what she wanted. "You never told me who you were working for or how you got caught," she finally said.

"It's probably better if you don't know." His voice came out harsher than he intended and he inwardly winced. "Just in case things don't go as planned."

She raised her eyebrows. "Are you going to let me in on these things you have planned?"

Her surprise dented his pride a little bit. He tried to sit up, to feel a little more in control. "You know the lay of the land, you have a contact on the outside that can extract us. We've got a window of time right now where we're alone. Let's make the most of it. Just point me in the right direction."

"It doesn't work like that." She neatly cut him off. "We're on the border of Afghanistan and Pakistan, the most dangerous part of the terrorists' thoroughfare between the two countries. No one asks questions and everyone carries a gun or an RPG. Even if we got farther than the armed guards around the court- yard, I don't have a vehicle waiting. It'll take time for an extrac- tion team to get here."

"Escape and evade. Surely you remember that class. The longer I'm at this temporary location, the likelier I am to be sent somewhere secure. I need to get out now while I've got the opportunity and head in the opposite direction of Pakistan."

She sat down in the wooden chair, and he knew by the look on her face she was going to say something he wouldn't like. "Colt, this *is* their secure place for prisoners. You're not the first and you won't be the last." She looked around the room. "They do terrible things here. People die."

He suppressed a shiver. In his mind, he'd always be able to resist anything that happened if he was captured, but now that he was faced with it, he wasn't so sure. There was nothing he could do now, though, but go forward. "I'll be all right."

The silence in the room lengthened as they both retreated into their own thoughts, but when they heard the approaching footsteps coming down the path, Brenna leaped into action. She quickly pulled the chair back to the side table and stood in the corner. "I'll do my best to at least let someone on the outside know you're here," she whispered. And then they both waited for the door to open.

The man who'd given him the needles the night before strode in. He glanced at Colt before his gaze settled on Brenna. Her eyes widened and while she quickly pulled her hijab over her hair and smoothed down the edges, Colt had still seen the hungry look on the other man's face as he stared at her. Colt flexed his free arm. If he needed to defend her, how long would it take to untie the other arm?

The man crossed to her corner and stood over her. She bowed her head. If Colt didn't know better, he would think she was a good servant, anxious to do this man's bidding. The guy spoke to her in Pashto, his tone harsh, but not cruel. She answered him back, her eyes on the floor. Colt had to admit, she was good. There was hardly even a trace of an accent. She sounded like a native.

The man crossed back to his bedside. "You are well enough for questioning." His English was heavily accented, but clear. Colt said nothing and the man cracked his knuckles. "By the end of today, I will know everything about you and your task force."

Colt could feel Brenna's eyes boring into the back of his head, but he kept his focus on the man in front of him. Something was off. His brow furrowed in confusion as he saw Colt's free arm and he turned to Brenna. Colt didn't have to speak fluent Pashto to know he was questioning her about it. The man took a step toward her, his voice getting louder with every word. Colt straightened as much as his position would allow.

"Hey," he said, wanting to draw the guy's attention away from her. Before he could blink, the man's fist crashed into Colt's jaw. Blinding pain shot through his head and the world went blissfully black once again.

CHAPTER SIX

Brenna couldn't breathe, her heart slamming against her ribs so hard she put her hand over it. She wanted to stay and make sure Colt was all right after that blow to the head, but Saabir had ordered her back to the kitchen with Aadela. She didn't have a choice, but turning her back on an injured Colt was the hardest thing she'd ever had to do. What was Saabir going to do to him?

She had to convince Aadela that they needed something at the market so she could contact her handler. Colt's time was limited and if they were going to have any chance of rescuing him, she had to get word out today. With her mind made up, she closed the door to the shack behind her and walked quickly up the path to the main house. She had to get to the market.

When she reached the kitchen, Aadela was nowhere to be found, but the pastries for the meat pies they were serving for dinner were on the counter. A plan started to form in Brenna's mind. This was her chance to create an excuse to go to the market. She quickly went to the spice cupboard and took down the cumin. It was Aadela's secret ingredient in making the pies that Saabir liked. She wouldn't serve them without it.

Knowing Aadela could be back any moment, Brenna retraced her steps to the door that led to the courtyard. Glancing behind her, she stepped out, going a few paces away into the garden. She sank down and quickly dug the best hole she could with just her hand. She couldn't pry off the top of the spice container, her hands were shaking so bad. *Breathe*, she told herself before she poured the contents into the hole and covered it up. Hiding the now empty container of cumin in the folds of her burka, she quietly went back inside.

Aadela was looking over the pastries and barely glanced up as she came into the kitchen. "The spices need to be mixed. Bring them to me," she said sharply.

That was close. Brenna went to stand in front of the spice cupboard and reached in, acting as if she were bringing down the cumin she already had in her hand. She held up the empty bottle. "But, madam, we are out of cumin."

Aadela's jaw dropped. "*Balaa*, how can that be?" She came to Brenna's side and took the spice container from her. "We cannot serve meat pie without it."

"Is there another spice we could substitute for it?" Brenna schooled her face into a neutral expression. Aadela had to think Brenna going to the market was her idea.

"No," Aadela snapped. "It must be cumin. You will hurry to the market before it closes to get more." She stared down at Brenna. "I'll expect you back in thirty minutes, no later. We have work to do."

She started to say yes in English, but caught herself and

answered in Pashto instead. *"Hao."* Speaking English to Colt had made her forget herself and that was something she could not do. She was a country girl from the mountains of Afghanistan- a slave in the household- not a Canadian girl worried about her first love being tortured.

Brenna went to her small broom-closet sized room two doors down from the kitchen. It only had a bed and a small chest in it, but at least it was her own space. She grabbed the blue burka she was required to wear when she went to market off the hook and pulled it over her head, quickly finding the mesh that went in front of the eyes. When she'd first worn it, she'd had difficulty fitting the cap on that held everything in place, but it was second nature now. The front of her burka ended around hip-level, so her hands were free to write a coded message on the back of a small piece of paper. She slipped it into the pocket of her pants and then arranged the burka over her clothing once again.

She hoped the new guard would be stationed at the door to take her to the market. The guards generally kept a fairly close eye on her and Aedala, but the new guard barely seemed to keep track of them at all. She needed that today. Sending a message on a day other than her appointed check-in was dangerous and she needed every break she could get.

Brenna walked toward the door, allowing herself a small smile from behind the mesh of her burka. New Guard was there near the entrance. "I need to go to the market," she told him, firmly back to being immersed in Pashto.

He nodded without a word and held the door open for her. It was still a little strange that she had to be accompanied whenever she went beyond the house gates. Passing information while under a guard's watch had taken a while to get used to, but the new guard not being particularly observant was like a little gift from the undercover mission gods. Hopefully her luck would hold, especially now.

He ushered her into the backseat of the older model Toyota. She arranged her burka around her feet and watched as he got into the driver's seat. "Aedala needs me back in thirty minutes so we must hurry," Brenna told him. He pressed on the gas a little harder and gravel sprayed behind him. No one in the house wanted to cross Aedala and he'd obviously learned that lesson well.

The afternoon was almost gone and the vendors would be packing up their market stalls soon. If she wanted to catch her liaison, Yar, before he left for the day, she'd need to be there in the next twenty minutes. She opened the window to get a small breeze, a little breath of air in the sticky heat. Yar had been a figurative breath of fresh air, a friendly face, a sympathetic ear whenever she could get far enough ahead of her guard to have a chance to chat on market day. But today she wouldn't be able to talk to him. She could only deliver the message and hope that Yar got it to the right people in time.

They parked on the southern edge of the market and she hurried to Yar's spice stall. Oddly, New Guard was close on her heels and Brenna hoped he wasn't becoming more vigilant on the one day she needed him to be oblivious.

The marketplace was long and narrow, with primitive wooden carts lining each side. Some had colorful sheets of material covering their produce and some were open to the sun and dirt. The open ones had to ask lower prices for their produce because it never looked good for long.

Brenna skirted around several groups of people still shopping and haggling with the vendors. The road that separated each side was drier than ever and the crowds were stirring up the dust as they moved. Thankfully, her burka filtered some of that out. She forged ahead with New Guard trailing behind her, feeling a sense of urgency as her allotted time ticked down. Getting to Yar's stall was going to be more difficult than ever, but at least the crowds would help her blend in.

She stopped in front of Yar and held a hand to her chest as she caught her breath.

"*Alaikum,*" she greeted him finally. "We have run out of cumin for the evening meal."

The guard turned away from her and Yar to look at the man dressed in a colorful *chapan* coat selling fruit in the next stall over. Now was her chance. She reached inside her pants pocket to put the note in her hand.

"You are in a hurry today, little one," Yar said. His mouth crinkled in a smile, and with his *pakol* hat set jauntily to the side, he looked a little like her grandpa in his favorite Tilley fedora. "I will get you the container, but you must rest a moment." He reached out to take her hand and Brenna was ready to pass the note in her palm.

"Thank you," she murmured. The note passed easily, as it had dozens of other times she'd done it. She relaxed. All she could do now was wait and hope.

When Yar stepped away to find her the cumin, she looked around his small stall. He was a simple man who was a common vendor. Yet, he wanted to help rid his country of men like Nazer and did what he thought necessary to do that. He'd agreed to help by being a liaison between her and those waiting on the other end for her reports. The lengths he was willing to go amazed her, but knew she had the same reasons for being here and trying to protect her countrymen as well.

Yar came back with a container nearly identical to the one Brenna had emptied. "My last one," he said. "You are lucky today."

Brenna smiled. That meant her message would go out immediately. Sometimes he wasn't able to send them for a day or two. Knowing that Colt's life could very well depend on the right people being informed of his whereabouts, Yar's news felt like fate was smiling on her today. "*Manana.*"

She settled the bill and joined her guard who was now bargaining with the fruit vendor for some apricots. Standing slightly behind him while he made his purchase, suddenly the day didn't seem so dark. Maybe everything really would be okay.

After a silent ride home from the market, the guard let her out at the front door, then parked the car around the side of the house. Brenna went immediately to the kitchen, flipping the face covering of the burka up over her cap so she could see.

Aaedela snatched the cumin from her. "I will mix the spices. You can start to clean up." There was no thank you or anything else beyond another order. Not that Brenna expected any thanks. After all these months of working with Aadela, Brenna had yet to hear her speak a kind word.

Brenna went to the sink and plugged it, pumping some of their precious water in to start soaking the dishes. She didn't want to be here doing dishes. She wanted to go to Colt's room and make sure he was all right and tell him the good news. The thought of Colt having to deal with Saabir's questioning any longer than he had to put a damper on the day. He wouldn't last long being groggy from the meds already. Hopefully a rescue would be mounted sooner rather than later so Saabir wouldn't get a chance to cause any more pain.

As if her thoughts had conjured him, Saabir appeared in the kitchen. "Bring me a large pail of cold water. Now."

Aadela let out a long drawn out sigh and nodded toward a pail in the corner. "Go," she told Brenna. "But hurry back or we'll never get dinner ready in time."

Brenna moved swiftly to the sink and pumped water into the pail. Lifting it out, she nearly spilled some on the floor, her pulse picking up at the thought of seeing Colt again. She tamped down her feelings as she made her way back outside, awkwardly carrying the heavy pail of water at her side. Her mind was racing with questions of why Saabir wanted the water. Was he trying to clear Colt's grogginess? Would he force his head down into the pail until he talked? There were so many possibilities, but none that would be pleasant for Colt, that was for sure.

Saabir held open the door for her as she carried the water in. "Put it near the bed," he instructed.

She did as she was told and was barely able to hold in a gasp as she looked at Colt. He was now bare from the waist up and there were fresh bruises on his face and abdomen. His hands were both pulled painfully above his head. The wound on his shoulder had a pool of blood underneath it. He was a mess.

She couldn't look away, her heart sinking to her feet. It was exactly what she'd feared. He was going to kill Colt. Brenna clenched her fists. She couldn't be the one to witness it.

Saabir wasn't paying attention to her anymore. He was busy

laying a cloth over Colt's face. Brenna knew what came next. Saabir would hold him down and pour the water over the cloth as the water filled Colt's sinuses and lungs. He wouldn't be able to breathe as he sucked in the water until he more or less drowned from it. Colt wouldn't be able to stand the agony of waterboarding in his condition.

Saabir was getting everything ready like this was something routine. The dim light put a shine on his head and Brenna started, her eyes taking in Saabir's form. He'd freshly shaved both his face and his head. In Saabir's world that meant he was preparing for battle and probably a suicide attack. Nazer had taught them that in order to be purified they had to shave before the event. Was the next attack closer than she'd thought? Or was his battle here with Colt? If she waited to find out, Colt would be dead.

Now was her moment of truth and she knew what she had to do.

No guards had been posted outside the shack, so she would only have Saabir to contend with. She was only going to get one chance to get Colt out of here. Brenna looked around the room. What could she use as a weapon? Saabir was nearly twice her size. The only thing readily available was the heavy glass pitcher still on the side table.

"You will tell me what I want to know," Saabir said as he bent to reach for the pail she'd brought in, hefting it like it weighed nothing.

Before she could over-think it, Brenna grabbed the pitcher and smashed it across the back of Saabir's head. The shattering sound seemed to echo through the room and glass went everywhere, some cutting her hand. Saabir had dropped like a rock.

She stepped around him and snatched the cloth off Colt's face. "Come on, we're getting out of here."

Colt groaned and closed his good eye. "Thank you."

She bent down and felt for a pulse in Saabir's neck. "Do you think I killed him?"

"If you didn't, let me up and I'll finish him off."

Her fingers felt a faint pulse. "We don't have time for that. If he wakes up, we're both dead." They had to go. Now.

She could hear someone shouting and knew a guard had been alerted. Her fingers were clumsy in her hurry as she tried to untie Colt's hands. He stood as quickly as he could, but still held on to the table for a few seconds, rubbing his wrists to try and get some circulation back. With his hands on his knees, he grabbed the needle from under the edge of the bed.

"Someone's coming, we have to leave." She pulled on Colt's arm.

"This will just take a second." He stabbed the syringe into Saabir's shoulder. "Let's make sure he stays down until we're far away from here."

She nodded and opened the door, looking up and down the path. So far it was empty, but guards were all around the perimeter of the house. It wouldn't be empty for long if they truly had been heard. How could she get them out of here? She needed a distraction. "This way," she told him, "but stay out of sight."

He closed the door behind them and even with his injuries he was able to stay close. She went to the side of the courtyard where there was a small corner hidden from the guard's view. "Wait here," she instructed as she motioned him to it. She hated to be separated, but it couldn't be helped and it would only be for a moment. Hopefully.

He nodded and gingerly leaned against the wall as he watched her go into the house. The second she was inside, she went to the dining room. No dishes were out on the table, so she had a little time before Aedela came in. Taking a lit candle, she waved it along the hem of the sheer curtains. The material caught fire quickly. She watched it take hold before she turned to leave. Noticing a *chapan*, the traditional Afghan coat men wore over baggy pants, sitting on the table, she grabbed it and put it under her arm. Colt would need something to wear and this was better than nothing.

Hoping New Guard was still at his post, she rushed to the front door. His slight frame stepped toward her when she cried out, "The curtains are on fire. Hurry! We need water!"

She nearly fell into his arms, sobbing. He caught her and as he lifted his arms to grab her shoulders, she took the keys to the car from his pocket. "I'm so afraid," she whimpered, carefully pulling the keys into the folds of her burka.

He patted her shoulder as he stood her up. "Go outside, but stay in the courtyard," he ordered. Other guards were coming in now, smelling the smoke.

She ran out the door and around to the side of the house to the blue gate that led to the courtyard. Her hand was slippery on the stolen key, the cut she'd received from the glass pitcher dripping blood. Dropping the *chapan*, she focused on using both hands to unlock the gate and finally wrenched it open.

She quickly bent to pick up the coat, then beckoned to Colt. "Come on," she said as she held up the car keys. "Time to go."

He didn't have to be asked twice and immediately headed

for the car parked near them. She handed him the *chapan*. "I know it's a coat, but you'll attract a lot less attention if you're wearing it."

Colt looked down at his bare torso and back at her. "Not bad. Thanks." He winced as he slipped it on.

She nodded, thinking the coat made him look dark and dangerous, exactly like the Special Forces operative he was. They'd need that knowledge if they were going to live through this.

He yanked open the driver's side of the car and held out his hands for the keys.

"You're in no shape to drive," she said immediately. "Besides, I know where we're going."

"Everyone will remember seeing a woman driving. We need to blend in." He looked back toward the house. "We don't have time to argue. Give me the keys."

She sighed and tossed him the keys, not wanting to admit he was right. If this was going to work, they needed to blend and that meant a woman was in the back behind the passenger seat. Frustrated at the inconvenience of it, she blew out a breath as she got in. "Go down the driveway and turn left." She directed him toward the town she'd come from an hour earlier. It felt like an eternity had passed since then. "Head straight until I tell you."

He followed her instructions and drove away from the compound as fast as he could without being too obvious. She hunched down a bit when another car approached, heading for the house. But she noticed a familiar shape in the back seat.

Nazer.

Brenna quickly pulled down her face covering and could

only hope the shadows from the sunset sufficiently hid Colt. Maybe the heavily tinted windows on Nazer's car were dark enough that he couldn't get a good look. She held her breath and waited for sixty seconds before turning around to watch his car. It seemed to speed up as it headed toward the house, which now had smoke curling out of the front door.

Colt must have seen him, too. He pressed on the gas pedal, obviously as anxious as she was to put distance between them and Nazer. Their missions were over. There was no coming back from this. All she needed to do now was get them out of the country safely. Her mind discarded Plan A of laying low and waiting for rescue. Plan B of just getting him to a military base and letting him find his own way wouldn't work either. Nazer would be searching for him, wanting revenge, and she couldn't risk Colt's re-capture. No, the only way was Plan C where both of them got extracted to a secure location.

She wiped her bloody hand on the edge of her burka as the car ate up the miles. Their only choice was to head for the closest village on the Afghan/Pakistan border that had a safe house with a SAT phone. She could call in their coordinates and get an extraction for two. Turning around one more time, she swept the road. No one was following them. Yet.

"Turn here."

Colt did as she asked and they headed east toward the Pakistan border. Plan C was going to be tricky, there was no getting around that. She certainly never thought she'd ever say that Pakistan might be the place to find safety, but it might be their only chance now.

CHAPTER SEVEN

Colt kept an eye on any cars that came near, but no one gave them a second glance. Escape couldn't have been that easy, could it? He glanced in the rearview mirror. Brenna hadn't said anything for the last fifteen minutes, but she was biting her lip, obviously deep in thought. Was she worried about extraction? What was the protocol?

"So, can you fill me in on the plan?" He leaned forward, trying to make sure his shoulder didn't touch the seat. His back felt like a thousand razor blades were being dragged across his skin and he was lightheaded. Beyond that, it was like all his strength had been zapped by whatever was in the syringe he'd been given. Hopefully the drug's effects would wear off sooner rather than later.

"I have a contact in a village near the border. We'll stay there until I can get extraction orders." She stared out the window as she spoke, but he couldn't figure out what she'd be looking at so intensely. The landscape was a sea of brown. The sunset had left some orangey brown streaks on the horizon, but it was getting dark. There wouldn't be much to see in a few more minutes. "We need to ditch the car in ten minutes or so. You able to walk?" She turned her head and met his gaze in the rearview mirror, waiting for his answer.

He wanted to say no, but he couldn't let her down. She was their only way out and if she said walk, he'd walk. "Sure." He'd just have to hope he didn't pass out. "How far?"

"A couple of miles." She leaned forward. "I'm sorry. I know you're hurting, but we need to cover our tracks."

"I understand." And he did. He'd just never felt like his body had been turned inside out, sliced into bits, and then shoved back together. Everything hurt. At least Brenna had stopped the waterboarding. There was no way to prepare for something like that and he didn't know how long he could have held out. "Thanks for helping me get out of there."

She reached forward and touched his uninjured shoulder. "I couldn't stand there and watch you suffer, Colt." Her voice was soft, but determined. She'd always had an iron will when something needed to be done and in this moment, he was more than grateful for that.

"I know it compromised your mission. I'm sorry about that." If he were in her shoes, he'd blame himself and he didn't want that for her.

"It's not your fault. You were right. As soon as you got to the house my mission was over." She looked out the window again, the encroaching darkness hiding her expression.

"Wait, did I just hear you say I was right?" He smiled, trying to lighten the mood a little. "This whole mess might have been worth it just to hear that."

She gave a low chuckle. "You might not say that if we don't get out of this."

"We'll get out, but are you sure Pakistan is our best bet? There are coalition military installations in Afghanistan that might work better." He put two hands back on the steering wheel and cracked the window a bit. Every time the car bounced over a pothole in the road, it made his body ache. He needed to focus on something other than the pain. A little breeze on his face wasn't much, but every bit helped.

"How did you know we're heading to Pakistan?" She sounded surprised.

"I've served a couple of tours in Afghanistan. I know my way around." He could see the mountain range ahead of them. "If I'm thinking right, that's the Khyber pass up ahead."

She made a little noise of approval. "I'm impressed. And you don't even have GPS with you." Leaning forward, she pointed ahead. "At the next curve in the road we ditch the car and hike into the village. It's not big, but we can lay low there until I can get word up the chain of command that we need immediate extraction. Keep going straight off the curve. There's a little indent in the vegetation. We can hide the car there."

He did as she said and pulled over. If he didn't know this little alcove was here, he never would have seen it. The perfect place to hide a car. "Should we cover it or something?"

"I think the darkness will hide it well enough until we can get to the safehouse." She walked around to his side of the car. "Are you sure you feel up to walking a couple of miles?"

"Do I have a choice?"

"Not really." She stepped closer. "But you can lean on me if you like."

He was tempted to, but there were already too many complications between them. Maybe it was best if he just tried to see how far he could make it on his own power. The slightly cooler night air felt good on his face and he was starting to feel more in focus. Walking would probably help the drugs to wear off. "I'll walk for a bit." He took a few steps and she fell into step beside him. "So, are you ever going to tell me who you're working for?"

"Classified." She turned her head toward him. "What about you?"

"Same."

She laughed, probably more out of courtesy than anything else, but it warmed him anyway. "Aren't we a pair?"

They were walking a few meters away from the road, but the thoroughfare was deserted. The only thing for miles was a lot of brush and uneven ground. He needed to step carefully, but couldn't resist looking up at the sky full of stars. "Reminds me of that time we took the ferry out to Wolfe Island." It had been a clear night like this, and he'd kissed her for the first time. "Do you remember?" Did she want to remember?

"Yeah." She didn't look at him and her footsteps quickened until she was a few steps in front of him. "I remember a lot of mist and water spray. I wouldn't mind some of that right about now."

He sighed inwardly. At least she had some positive memories, but was she deliberately silent on what they'd shared? Had she truly put everything between them behind her? His steps slowed as he let her put more physical distance between them. "Did you ever dream we'd meet up again in Afghanistan?"

She turned and the moonlight illuminated her look of resignation as she tilted her head toward him. "To be honest, I didn't think we'd ever see each other again."

Her words stung. She really had made a clean break and not looked back. *What am I doing hanging on to the past?* He nodded, hoping she hadn't thought he was pushing for a reconciliation or something. Seeing her again in these circumstances had just thrown him, that's all. "I'm sure as soon as we're extracted we won't cross paths again." But would that be true? Did he want it to be?

It didn't matter what he wanted. With an inward sigh he caught up to her. She hadn't planned on seeing him again. What could be more clear than that? He looked down at her, his eyes traveling down to the strange way she was holding her forearm. In the dim light, he could see the dark shadows of blood streaking down her hand. "You're hurt." He gently took her elbow, raising her arm so he could see it more clearly.

"I cut my hand when I smashed the pitcher." She tried to twist her head around so she could see the wound, but it was hard to see in the darkness. "I think it's stopped bleeding now."

His stomach twisted at how big the bloodstain was. "Why didn't you say something sooner?"

"What would I have said? Hey, I've got a little cut on my hand." She tried to pull her hand away, but he held it fast.

"It's more than a little cut." Her hands used to be soft, but now he could feel the roughness of the skin, the calluses that testified she'd worked hard. He looked down, his gaze locking on her. As much as he didn't like the burka and hijab she'd been forced to wear, with only her face showing, everything else faded away. She'd always had the most expressive eyes and he'd teased her once that she'd never be good undercover because anyone could read her feelings the second they looked in her eyes. Obviously he'd been wrong. Very wrong. Unspoken words crackled in the energy around them and he had the overwhelming urge to pull her to him and kiss her.

She bent forward as if she could read his thoughts and his heart sped up. Touching her cheek to his briefly, she took a step back and looked down. "I'm fine, Colt."

He let her hand go, the feel of her soft skin branded on his. "Bren." Her name sounded strangled and he cleared his throat. "Do you have any regrets?" He really needed to shut up, but he couldn't help himself. He had so many unresolved feelings running around in his head that he knew weren't an effect of the drug.

Brenna turned to move away, but he gently took her elbow. She looked up at him, her eyes shining. "I have a lot of regrets, Colt. Too many to count."

Her answer made his tongue thick. Did she mean about them? "Would you go back and change things if you could?"

She shook her head and backed away another step. "We need to get going or we'll miss our ride."

She was right. This wasn't the time to talk about the past. He pulled the *chapan* coat closer to him. "It's getting colder, don't you think?"

Drawing her brows together, she reached up to put the back of her hand against his forehead. "I hope you're not coming down with a fever." She put her hands on her hips. "If you're hurting or need to rest, you have to tell me."

"Like you told me about your hand?" He quirked a brow.

She let out a breath of frustration. "Fine. From now on,

you're going to tell me when you're hurting and I'll do the same."

He wanted to smile at the picture she made standing in the middle of Afghanistan dressed in a burka, ordering him around like a small general who expected to be obeyed. "Deal."

She turned and started walking again and he followed her. His body was starting to get into a rhythm as they walked, but after the first mile, exhaustion set back in while Brenna didn't even seem to be breathing hard. Raging inside at his weakness, he just concentrated on putting one foot in front of the other. Those drugs wouldn't beat him. He ground his teeth together. Left, right. Left, right. *Not much farther*, he told himself. *Just keep going.*

He couldn't keep up. She turned, and with a shake of her head, walked back and put her arm around his waist. "Stubborn man," she said as she helped him forward.

As tired as he was, he could still appreciate how well she fit against his side. He pulled her closer, the feel of her strength and softness giving him an extra burst of energy. "Tell me how you really feel."

"Okay, I will. I know you're trying to be all I-got-this, but I know what you've been through in the last twenty-four hours. Let me help you."

"You can be so irritating sometimes." But she was right and they both knew it. He let himself lean on her a little more. "Thanks, Bren."

She squeezed his waist. "You're welcome."

They didn't talk much after that. Both of them were concentrating on managing the terrain and keeping Colt upright. Finally the village came into sight and Colt breathed a sigh of relief. He wanted to sit down. Lie down. Be anywhere but upright. "We made it."

"Not quite yet." They trudged to the outskirts of the village, houses on every square inch of ground, mashed together with clotheslines running between them. Open sewage and trash ran down the middle of the street, the smell enough to make Colt gag. She nudged him down an alley. "This way."

Brenna kept them in the shadows as they took the twists and turns between houses, but the entire village was asleep. There weren't any night sounds, though, and it made the hair on the back of Colt's neck stand up. What if this was a trap?

Finally they stopped at a large pile of rubble looming in front of them, blocking the way. "This is supposed to be a straightaway," Brenna said, staring at the blockage. "The door is supposed to be right here."

"Obviously that's changed. Doesn't look like there's any way over it, either." He pushed off her shoulder to lean against one of the broken pieces of concrete. "Now what?"

"We'll have to find a way around it." She was biting her lip again, obviously going over options in her mind.

A small metal door swung inward near the side of the blockage and they both whipped around. A small man stepped out, his hands in the air. "Can I help you?"

He spoke in Pashto, his eyes on Brenna.

"I'm trying to find the healer who would help a woman in need," she said, standing slightly in front of Colt as she spoke. Was she shielding him? His gaze swung back to the smaller man in front of them. Normally, Colt wouldn't have any trouble if it came down to a fight, but right now, his grandma could probably take him.

"I am the healer who is a friend to women." He smiled, his white teeth gleaming in the moonlight. His voice dropped to a whisper. "You are the professor, yes? I am Duke." He seemed pleased with his pronunciation of the English words. He motioned them forward. "Come, come. I can help you," he said, his eyes darting toward the end of the alley. Voices floated their direction and there was no way to tell if it was friend or foe. "Hide." He motioned to the clay-colored building behind him.

Brenna didn't hesitate. The guy must have said the right words. Colt squinted, looking at the rubble surrounding him. Maybe he could just sit here. Be a lookout. Anything except stand again. But Brenna was already squeezing through the doorway and he groaned inwardly as he straightened.

When he stepped inside, his nose was immediately assaulted with the scent of spices. They were in a storage room of sorts, with herbs and food items hanging from the ceiling, the floor boasting a dozen sacks neatly stacked halfway up the wall. Their new friend Duke stood near the door, silently watching them.

Colt sank to the ground near the largest stack of sacks. Brenna moved over and crouched beside him. "Are you all right?"

"I made it." And that felt like a huge accomplishment. All he wanted to do was close his eyes.

She ran a hand over his forehead again and glanced over her shoulder at Duke. "My friend here is hurt. Do you have any bandages? Medicine that might help?"

Colt gave in and closed his eyes before Duke could answer. It was soothing having Brenna near, her hands on his face. Even with the predicament they were in, something inside him said they could get out of this if they'd just stick together.

"Yes, yes, I get them for you." Duke left the room and Brenna leaned over him, picking up the edge of the *chapan* to look at his shoulder. Colt opened his eyes, his skin tingling from the light touch of her fingers running over his collarbone.

"We're going to get you fixed up." She smiled and his pulse picked up. Even with the dirt of the day on her face, she was beautiful. Was he imagining the tenderness in her touch? There was a time they'd been inseparable, finishing each other's sentences, and even looking forward to a life together. Why had he let her walk away?

He reached out an unsteady hand and let his thumb trail over her jaw. "You're so beautiful." His body might as well have been weighed down with lead, though. He couldn't control the fatigue flowing over him and his hand dropped to his side.

"Take it easy." She ran a hand over his brow and he closed his eyes again. "I've got you covered."

And he knew she did.

CHAPTER EIGHT

Brenna took off her burka and balled it up as a makeshift pillow for Colt. She didn't want to wake him up, but Duke had come back with some pain medication and medical supplies. The sooner Colt was treated, the less chance there was of infection. She gently shook his shoulder. "Hey, I need to get you bandaged up. Can you turn over?"

Colt made a small moan in the back of his throat, but did as she asked. "What's the plan?" he asked when he was settled on his other side.

"We're waiting for contact. You've still got time to rest." She handed him some pills and a cup of water before pulling the *chapan* down over his shoulder, careful to keep him on his side. "It's ibuprofen. I know it's not much, but you look like you could use something to take the edge off."

He took the pills from her and swallowed the water in one

gulp. "You're one to talk." He looked up at her with his good eye and reached out for her hand. "How's the cut?"

"Bandaged. Almost as good as new." But not immune to the flutter of nerves flying over her at his touch, making her words sound rushed and breathless. She didn't pull her fingers away, though.

"Glad to hear it," he murmured.

He was still staring at her and she squirmed a little under his gaze. With her free hand, she reached up to touch her hair. The bun she'd put in this morning was nearly gone now. "I probably look a mess. With this heat, I'm lucky I didn't melt in that burka."

"Just take it down," Colt advised. "Or let me."

Her hand stilled. Did he remember how he used to do that for her? Or was it the drugs talking? The thought of his hands in her hair stirred up the butterflies in her belly again. It was tempting, but she needed to keep control and that might undo her resolve. "I'll just pin it up again." She pulled her fingers away from his, the memory of him taking down her hair while he kissed her neck making her flush. Maybe she should leave it down to hide that, but she'd never been able to hide much from him. He read her so well. She quickly redid her hair into a messy bun. Yep. It was definitely better to have it up, out of her face and out of his hands.

He watched her finish and when she was done, he slowly ran a hand over his face, as if smothering his own thoughts. "Where's our friend Duke?"

The change of subject didn't dispel the memories running through her mind or the cocoon of familiarity between them. But it was probably a good thing to steer their thoughts to the task at hand. "He's making you a poultice of some sort. Being a healer and all, he felt like it was his responsibility." She didn't want Duke to go to any trouble, but he was so eager to help she couldn't say no.

"Well, at this point, I'm willing to try anything." He grimaced and tried to adjust his position, in obvious pain.

"I noticed you've got quite a few scars." Her voice was quiet. What if he didn't want to talk about them?

"Despite what that might look like, I'm good at my job." He adjusted her burka under his head.

"A few close calls, though?"

"Yeah." He looked over at her. "I guess your new scar will be joining the other one on your hand?"

She laughed. "I can't believe you remembered that." Holding up her bandaged hand, the white line across the top knuckles of her fingers was clearly visible. "My mom never let me live that down. The one time I went skating without gloves, fell, and got ran over by a runaway guy on skates."

"You're lucky you didn't lose a finger." Colt smiled. "Moms always know."

"Believe me, she didn't hesitate to say I told you so." She sobered. "My scars seem pretty small compared to yours."

He shrugged his uninjured shoulder. "I did a few tours with JTF2 and got in some sticky situations. I always managed to find my way out."

"And we'll get out of here, too." She should have gotten him out sooner and the guilt was starting to gnaw at her. She pushed it away. *I did the best I could.* "Wait, did you say you're not with JTF2 anymore? Who are you here with?"

Colt puffed out a groan of frustration at his slip. "Where is

Duke with that poultice?" he muttered, looking anywhere but at her.

She shook her head. "You might as well just tell me."

"Are you going to talk about how you got the code name of Professor for this op? Or did you make a career detour I don't know about?" He rested his good arm on a sack in front of him.

She knew he was changing the subject, and he had every right to. He'd already said who he worked for was classified and she needed to respect that. She cleared her throat, intending to apologize, but her throat seemed to dry up a little more every time she looked at him. How could he look so relaxed with a burka for a pillow and a sack for a makeshift bed? "It's a boring story."

"So were most of my professors." He grinned.

She liked the teasing glint in his eye. The years they'd been apart seemed to melt away. "Hey, are you implying I'm boring?"

He looked at their surroundings and then back at her. "Um, we're holed up in a storage room in Afghanistan after escaping from one of the most wanted terrorists in the world. I'd say that's the opposite of boring."

She laughed. "Good point, but it's a long story and I shouldn't talk about it anyway." And if she told him, it would seem like she was bragging or something.

"I bet I can guess. They found out your test scores. You're someone's tutor? You like to lecture? Am I close?" He smiled at her exasperated exhale. "I would have given you a name like Sunshine or Duchess."

"Sunshine? Really?" That made her feel good. No one on her team would have given her those names. She was all business when working, with no time for anything personal. Her code names always reflected that. "It wasn't any of those things. I made a few mission assessments and when I explained my theories to the team, they gave me the name."

"I could see you as a professor, actually." He looked up at her with his good eye, although the swelling was going down on his other one. "And it would be safer than your current profession."

"You don't get to comment on that." She shook her head, her good mood dissipating at his words. "I can take care of myself. And you, too, apparently. I got us here, didn't I?"

"Yes, you did." His voice was quiet. "I'm sorry. It's none of my business."

"I shouldn't have asked who you worked for, either." The air of camaraderie was gone, replaced with uncomfortable silence. Why had she pushed him about his job? Frustration bubbled up inside her. This was work and she needed to act like it, but her reaction to Colt's reappearance in her life had thrown everything off.

Duke poked his head into the room and Brenna was glad for the interruption.

"I have poultice for you." He walked across the room with a small bowl that smelled terrible.

Colt pulled back when a got a whiff of it. "What's in that?"

"Many things, many things." Duke squatted next to him. "We will put it on your bruises. It will draw the heat and pain out of your body."

"I'm all for that." He twisted his shoulders, and wrapped his arms around a sack, baring his back to them. With a little bit better lighting, Brenna could see the extent of his scars. There were burns, cuts, and road rash. A few odd shapes could have come from knives and there was one that was definitely a bullet wound. It made her catch her breath to realize how close Colt had come to death. She wrapped her arms around herself. He was strong, she'd always known that, but those scars proved it.

Duke began slathering the foul-smelling stuff on Colt with a small Popsicle-type stick. His body tensed, so she knew Duke's touch, as gentle as it was, hurt him. And the mixture stunk so bad it made Brenna's eyes water. But she didn't move from his side. He wasn't going to go through this alone. Not this time.

She watched Duke work, whistling as he dipped into the bowl again and again until Colt's torso was covered with it.

Once it was applied, Duke stood back to survey his work. "You sleep now."

"Thank you." He eyed the smaller man as he settled back against the sacks. "I hope I'm not being rude, but can I ask what your real name is?"

Duke didn't hesitate. "It's Yousef, but I love John Wayne. He is The Duke." He straightened and puffed out his chest, hooking his thumbs into imaginary belt loops on his baggy pants. "Take 'er easy there, pilgrim," he said in a heavily accented John Wayne voice.

Brenna smiled at his impression. "You've got him down pat."

Yousef bent his head in appreciation of her compliment. "Thank you, thank you. You are very kind. Someday I want to go to America and see where John Wayne was born." He moved back toward the doorway, still watching Colt and Brenna, when he suddenly froze. "Do you hear that?"

Brenna held her breath, her ears tuned to every sound. "What?" She'd gotten too comfortable and let her guard down.

If they'd been found because of her negligence, she'd never forgive herself.

"Someone is coming." Yousef put the bowl on the nearest barrel and started throwing the sacks in front of Brenna and Colt. "We must make it look as if I have just received a delivery and have not yet stacked it. Burrow in between the sacks and hide."

Colt sat up so Brenna could slide out from behind him and help Yousef with the sacks. They hid Colt first, making sure he was well-protected. "I hate being useless," he grumbled. "The ibuprofen's working and I feel more like myself. I can help."

"We're almost done." Brenna started another carefully placed, but unstacked, spot for herself.

"How did they find us?" Someone was knocking on the door and Brenna lay down a few feet from Colt.

"That's what I'd like to know," she said grimly. Yousef had gone to answer the door and she sent up a silent prayer for all of them.

"Do we have a contingency plan?" Colt whispered. "If not, maybe Yousef can make some more poultices and we can kill them with the smell."

She couldn't help herself, she chuckled at the image and some of the tension left her body. In a way that made no sense, somehow in this madness it felt good to have him with her. Now if only they could get out alive.

With only a small space left open for her mouth and nose, she concentrated on survival breathing. Slow. Steady.

Angry voices filled the hallways, getting louder. She lay there, trying to count footfalls to see how many men they would be up against if they had to fight their way out. She hoped it wouldn't come to that. Their hiding place was good, Brenna just needed to trust that.

The footfalls stopped and Yousef said fearfully, "I'll give you what you want. Please, don't hurt my family."

Brenna heard the slide of a knife being taken out of its sheath. She closed her eyes. It was all over.

CHAPTER NINE

Every muscle in Colt's body was tense. He knew he couldn't do a lot if their hiding place was found, but he'd go down fighting if it meant Brenna would have a chance to get away.

The voices in the storeroom drew closer and Colt forced himself not to react. Two sets of footsteps were only steps away from their hiding spot, but Colt couldn't see them.

"I'm here to collect your taxes, and I know you got another shipment in. It's time to pay or you know what will happen." The voice was nasally and rough, like the man had just come out of a dust storm and hadn't cleared his throat. Some of Colt's tension drained away. The guy wanted taxes. It wasn't about them or Nazer.

"I'll bring the poppy to the pre-arranged place tomorrow. I've never been late since we made our arrangement." Yousef's voice didn't waver and Colt was proud of him, especially considering if he were caught harboring two foreigners, he would most likely be killed. Colt moved slightly to the left, trying hard not to move around too much on his back, but he needed to get a visual on the newcomer.

The second he got eyes on the newcomer, he kicked the sacks near where Colt was hiding. Colt felt the reverberation, but didn't feel like he was in danger of discovery.

"Our agreement was you would provide the elders with the best poppy to keep them happy and your family alive. They are not happy. They want their portion now." He stepped closer to Brenna's hiding place and Colt nearly stopped breathing when he saw the knife in the man's hand. If he started picking up any of the sacks or slicing them open, she'd be exposed.

"I'll bring it first thing tomorrow. I want them happy." Yousef was also moving toward Brenna's location. Was he trying to get between her and whoever this guy was? It was hard to tell. He held still and trusted Yousef.

"We'll be expecting you." The room was silent for a heartbeat, then they both started moving toward the door. "Don't be late," the man said as a parting shot, pointing his knife at Yousef's face before his footsteps faded away. Yousef shut the door behind them.

Colt expelled a sigh of relief. That was close. He waited another sixty seconds before he dared to speak. "You okay?" he whispered to Brenna.

She started to move the sacks off of her and he followed her lead. "Yeah." When her shoulders were free she sat up, her white shirt stark against the dark brown sacks. "I thought it was all over for a minute there."

Yousef came back into the room and sank down to the floor

near Colt. "I'm so sorry. I didn't expect him to see my light. Careless of me to leave it burning."

"Who was that guy?" Colt asked.

"He's the sheriff of the village." Yousef straightened his *pakol* hat on his head. Usually those hats looked like two large fluffy pancakes perched atop the man's head, but Yousef's was completely flat. Both him and his hat looked like the air had been sucked out of them. "If you don't grow opium poppy on your land, the Taliban demands you pay them a tax to allow you to grow something else. For me, I must pay in special poppy since I have a supplier in the north that the elders like." He wouldn't meet their gaze and his shoulders slumped. "I do what I must to keep my family safe."

"You've refused before, haven't you?" Brenna asked softly.

Yousef nodded, still looking at the floor. "They beat me until I was unconscious and took my wife and son. I didn't see them for three days. When they were brought back to me, I promised to pay." He lifted his head, looking between the two of them. "That is why I help people like you. I want these men out of power. I want my country to finally have peace."

Colt's gut tightened as he looked at Yousef. He was doing what he had to do to protect his family, but at the same time he was working to make the world a better place for them. It was humbling. "You're a good man, Yousef."

"Thank you." He bowed slightly. "Now we must get you out safely." He handed Brenna a SAT phone. "You will only have a few minutes to make contact and the coverage is better on the balcony."

She took the phone without comment and stood. "Lead the way."

"I'm coming, too." Colt stood slowly, trying to keep any pain from his face. The poultice and ibuprofen had made things a bit better, but his body was crying out for rest. He'd make time for that later. Right now, he wasn't about to let Brenna out of his sight.

Yousef led them to a narrow set of stairs near the front of the house. "Go to your right and through that door. There is a small balcony that isn't easily seen from the street."

Brenna nodded and started up the stairs with Colt right behind her. The staircase was nearly the width of his shoulders, the stairs steep. It definitely wasn't made to fit a man his size. Colt glanced back at Yousef, still standing at the bottom of the stairs. Was he going to come with them? He hesitated a moment more, but then turned back toward the storage room. Apparently he trusted them to figure things out.

They went through the door Yousef had indicated and crossed the empty room. Brenna's staccato footsteps as she marched through the room in silence was so unlike her it was making him a little nervous. Was there something she wasn't telling him? "So what's the protocol? Will you be talking to someone live or just entering codes?"

"I blew the mission so, yeah, someone's going to pick up." Her voice was terse and she didn't look back as she continued on toward the balcony doors.

He reached for her arm. There was no way he could let that go. "I'm sorry, okay? I know you blew the mission to save me and I'll always be grateful for that."

She pulled the SAT phone to her chest, her expression softening. "I don't regret it, but I don't know if my superiors will see it the same way."

"They might think that letting me die was a small price to pay for finding out where Nazer is going to strike next." He dropped her arm. It was understandable, part of the business they were in, but it didn't mean he had to like it. "I don't want to get you in trouble."

"I'm way past trouble." She moved around him to the balcony. "And we don't have a lot of time."

He followed her as she carefully opened the door and slipped out, keeping as much to the shadows as she could. She pressed the numbers and held the phone close to her ear. "63848, the Professor needs a ride home." She listened for a moment. "The students are still in class." Brenna let out a sigh. "Understood."

She ended the call and slumped against the wall. Colt wanted to slip an arm around her, tell her it would be okay, but he didn't think she'd welcome that right now. "That didn't sound too bad. Are we all set?"

"Yeah. I got off easy over the phone. But now we're headed to the principal's office." A smile ghosted across her lips. "And the principal is a tough cookie."

"So are you." Colt reached out and traced her cheek with his thumb. "It's going to be okay. I'll do anything I can to help you explain."

She leaned into him and his heart tripped a bit as he eased his arms around her. She went up on tiptoe, possibly to avoid the smell of the poultice he had on, but part of him wanted to believe that she wanted to be as close to him as he wanted to be to her. His hold tightened and it felt so familiar, so right. He kissed the top of her head, but she stiffened and quickly pulled away.

"Um, thanks, Colt." She ran a hand over her hair, and avoided his eyes, fiddling with the phone in her hand.

He berated himself for getting lost in the moment, letting what was familiar trump what was right for the here and now. His hands dropped to his side. "No problem."

"It's been a long day for all of us. We better get going." Fumbling with the door, she finally got it open and went back inside the house without looking back.

He sighed and followed, her words echoing in his head, *"I have a lot of regrets, Colt. Too many to count."* Obviously leaving him six years ago wasn't one of them. Although he'd probably added another one to her list with that embrace on the balcony.

He allowed himself a moment of frustration as he lifted his head to the ceiling. With their history and the fact that she'd saved his life today, his feelings for her were a jumbled mess. There was no time to sort it out, though, until they were safely back in friendly territory without terrorists on their trail. But resolving his feelings for her had just moved up on his priority list.

Brenna didn't waste any time heading back downstairs. She wasn't waiting for him and he watched her disappear around the corner. His kiss had obviously spooked her, but she'd been the one to initiate the hug. He didn't know what to think, but one thing was clear, she didn't have a problem leaving him behind. But maybe that was a good reminder. She'd broken his heart before and if he didn't want that to happen again, he should probably keep his distance.

When he made it back to the storage room, Yousef and Brenna were talking in rapid Pashto. This was the part of Brenna she wanted everyone to see—take-charge and able to hold her own. It was in her private moments with him, when she'd been soft and vulnerable, laughing and carefree, that made her extraordinary. Those were the moments he treasured the most. He had to put those memories away, though. From her reaction upstairs, she definitely didn't want him to go there or see her as anything other than the capable undercover agent she was.

Yousef handed her a canteen, which she took, and then he gave her a bag. She hesitated on that one, but finally took it before she turned to Colt. "We've only got a few hours and we need to get closer to the Pakistani border."

"What's the plan for extraction?" He probably should have been asking for those details instead of thinking of her in his arms.

"Trust me." She gave him a broad smile as if she knew he would hate that answer and then bowed to Yousef. "Thank you so much for your help."

"Remember the instructions for the poultice. Be safe." He bowed to both of them and when he straightened, he hooked his finger near where a belt loop would be if he were wearing a belt. "Saddle up," he said in his John Wayne voice.

Colt raised his hand in goodbye and said the only John Wayne quote he knew. "We're burning daylight."

Yousef's eyes brightened. "That was one of my favorites of his movies."

Colt just smiled, hoping Yousef didn't ask him anything else about it. He didn't actually recall the name of the movie and had pulled that quote out of his memory bank. "Thanks again, Yousef. For everything"

Brenna was waiting impatiently by the door. For someone

who wasn't looking forward to going to the "principal's office" she was in a hurry. They left out the small door they'd come in. The alley was still as dark and blocked with rubble as it had been when they'd arrived. Were they going back the way they'd come?

"Hey, you don't have to carry that smelly poultice bag around. I don't want you to have any extra baggage. Just leave it here." He already felt like he wasn't pulling his own weight in their escape plan. Watching her lug around that poultice bag wouldn't make him feel any better.

Brenna's step was lighter without the burka on, and she was already a dozen steps ahead of him before she turned her head to answer. "You don't want to hurt his feelings, do you? Besides, *he'd* smell it and know we ditched it. He is sure it's going to draw your pain out."

"Oh, it draws the pain out all right. You can't feel the pain because you are crying from the stench." The clothing he was wearing would have to be burned. There was no way they were getting the stink out of it. Obviously Brenna didn't mind it much, though, since she'd never mentioned anything up on that balcony. *Back to the balcony again.* He needed to stop thinking about it.

She waited for him to catch up, a hand on her hip as she watched him. When he was next to her, she slung the bag Yousef had given her over her shoulder. "Quit being such a baby. It seemed to help."

He shrugged. Carefully so as to not hurt his shoulder. "Yes, ma'am. Whatever you say ma'am."

"And don't you forget it." Her eyes narrowed into a good-natured glare before she turned down the alley again. The strain that was between them had dissolved or at least been sidelined and Colt wasn't going to question it. She was obviously trying to put the complications between them behind her and he would do the same.

He followed close as she stayed near the buildings, all of his senses on alert. There had been too many missions where everything seemed quiet, right before they were lit up with enemy fire. He didn't even relax once they were clear of the village since they were headed toward the mountainous region near the Pakistan border. This particular area had about as many terrorist hideouts as there were lights on the Vegas strip.

"We've only got a small window before it's too light for a safe extraction. Are you going to be okay if we pick up the pace?" She stepped over a large piece of brush, glancing back at him.

Colt's mind protested any further punishment, but he nodded. "No problem." He could do this.

Her stride lengthened and he gave her a smile as he matched it. The sky was starting to lighten, making the dusty terrain and underbrush a little easier to navigate. Colt was glad he still had his boots and that Brenna was wearing sturdy, sensible shoes.

He tried to keep up with her, but after forty minutes that seemed like hours, Colt had to raise his hand. "I need to stop for a minute."

He bent over, his hands on his thighs. The stink of the poultice still lingered and he couldn't pull in a breath without smelling it, but he had to admit, it had helped. He was grateful the pain was less, but he still hurt with every step.

Brenna carefully put a hand on his shoulder. "We're almost there, I promise. You okay?"

"Not really." He was starting to feel dizzy. "How close are we?" Taking a risk, he set his feet and turned his head toward her. Everything spun for a moment, but she finally came into focus.

Her eyes were on the medium-sized mountain directly in front of them. "Probably only a half mile more." She gave him the canteen. "Drink the rest of it. We're almost there."

He gratefully took the water and took every last drop. The urge to sit down was overwhelming, but knew if he did, he wouldn't be getting back up. "I can do a half mile." He wiped his mouth and straightened. "Like a walk in the park, eh?"

She took his arm and laid it across her shoulders. "You can lean on me, you know."

She sounded unsure of his reaction, and to be frank, he didn't know how he felt about the feelings that their proximity had stirred up again, especially after the scene on the balcony. He gave her a quick squeeze, but pulled back. "Thanks, I think I've got it."

He thought he saw a shadow of hurt flash across her face at his words, but he might have been mistaken. If he had, it was gone now, replaced by the professional blank face every under-cover agent had to perfect out in the field. He turned away, trying to get that same look on his own face. Hurting Brenna wasn't his intention, but he had to get hold of his emotions when it came to her. Too many things were reminding him of how good it had once been between them. How much he'd admired her, loved her.

He moved forward, determined to put a little distance between them. "We don't want to miss our ride. We should go."

They walked in silence after that, the awkwardness between

them as heavy as the humidity that was gathering the closer they got to sunrise. Brenna finally stopped in a fairly flat area and looked skyward. As if on cue a Merlin helo came into view, coming straight toward their position. Colt watched the pilot expertly land on the narrow strip of ground available to them at the base of the mountain, and within seconds Colt and Brenna were running toward it.

As they climbed aboard, the thwack of bullets hitting their mark echoed through the helo. "Get in and get down!" Colt shouted. The poultice bag slipped from Brenna's shoulder onto the ground, but he grabbed her arm. "Leave it."

They barely had time to strap in before the helo attempted a tumultuous liftoff. The hail of bullets wasn't letting up. "Keep low," the pilot shouted.

Colt looked around them to pinpoint where the fire was coming from. A small rise up the mountain in front of them flashed as more gunfire sounded. "Over there!" he pointed.

The co-pilot nodded. "We've got it."

Even with all the noise surrounding them, Colt didn't miss the man's British accent. But before Colt could think anymore on it, the helo was returning fire. Maneuvering off the field and away from the surprise attack, the helo rose up, getting a better angle for her shots. The insurgents seemed undeterred, sending another volley toward them. The co-pilot turned toward them to make himself heard. "Sit tight, I don't think they're done with us yet."

Colt gave him the thumbs up, just as the familiar whine of a surface to air missile screeched through the air. The pilot shouted, "Hold on! We've got incoming!"

CHAPTER TEN

B renna gripped the sides of her seat. Intellectually she knew that the Merlin helo was equipped for these sorts of situations, but the fact was, a missile was coming for them and they very well may get hit. There wouldn't be a chance for any type of hard landing, unless you counted crashing into the mountains below. She glanced over at Colt. He was leaned forward, bracing for impact.

"Chaff deployed," the pilot said as he and his co-pilot pressed buttons and flipped switches like a choreographed dance. Explosions sounded behind them and Brenna instinctively pulled into a brace position. The roller-coaster ride lasted for several minutes before the co-pilot turned around so Colt and Brenna could hear him.

"We're heading to base." The smile on his face was enough for relief to flood through Brenna. They'd made it. It was over.

She glanced at Colt. He didn't seem quite as elated as she

was that their extraction had been successful, but she knew it could be the exhaustion. He couldn't have lasted much longer out there. His body had been through enough and he needed more than the poultice she'd been able to give him to heal some of those wounds. Hopefully a doctor would be available when they landed.

"Do you think that was Nazer's men?" Colt asked, looking over at her.

She shrugged. "This mountain range is known to harbor all sorts of criminals and terrorists. They could have just seen the helo and wanted the prestige of bringing it down."

She held Colt's eyes for a moment, wishing she'd handled things differently. Her professional life and personal life had never collided before, she'd made sure of that. But now everything was blurred and it was overwhelming. She needed some time to figure things out, but she couldn't seem to find the words to tell him that. So she'd run away, the worst possible thing she could have done, given their history. But there was no going back.

That hug probably hadn't meant anything to him anyway. He was just being kind to a friend who'd save his life. That's all. She was thinking too much about the feel of his kiss in her hair, when she should be concentrating on Nazer. If those were his men, they were in trouble. She needed a clean getaway so they could regroup and make a new plan for stopping his next attack.

Folding her hands in her lap and fiddling with the bandage on the end of her fingers, she looked down at the landscape below them. No matter who had shot at them, Nazer was still out there. He was going to hurt a lot of innocent people and she'd thrown away her chance to stop that from happening. But she couldn't regret saving Colt. Having his death on her conscience would have been too much to bear.

"ETA in ten," the co-pilot said. She nodded as her stomach twisted into knots. Ten minutes before she'd have to explain herself and why she'd scrubbed the mission. It wasn't long enough to find the words that needed to be said.

"Hey, you okay?" Colt asked, leaning toward her.

For one brief second she wanted to reach out and hold his hand, to feel that steadiness in him that had always calmed her. She hadn't even known she missed that. It cemented in her mind exactly why she hadn't hesitated to get him out no matter what the cost. Her hand started to reach out for his as if on its own accord, but she snatched it back. What was she thinking? He wouldn't welcome her touch. Hadn't he pulled away from her when she'd offered to let him lean on her? *Get it together.* "Yeah, I'm fine. Just thinking about how I'm going to explain all this."

Colt furrowed his brow as if he knew she wasn't being entirely truthful and he was trying to figure out what she was thinking. Thankfully, he wasn't a mind-reader. If he knew how much she'd been thinking about their past, and how his nearness had brought all those old feelings rushing back, he'd probably run the other direction. She'd broken his heart and there wasn't anything she could do to change that. She had to accept that they'd never be anything more than colleagues caught in a crazy war on terror. Their job descriptions didn't permit anything more than that.

By the time they landed at the black site, Brenna had a pretty good idea of what she wanted to say to her boss. Hopefully it would be enough. She was holding tight to the thought that there would be another opportunity to get close to Nazer. There had to be. Until then, they'd figure something out and she'd do anything she could to help.

A medic met them at the landing site and reached for Colt. "This way, Captain."

"No way," he said to the medic, then turned to Brenna. "I'm staying with you. We'll explain this together."

"Go get fixed up. I'm a big girl." She tried to give him a smile, but she knew it probably wasn't as convincing as she needed it to be. "Don't worry about me. I'll take care of myself."

Throwing those words in his face probably wasn't the best idea. When he'd realized she was breaking up with him five years ago, he'd asked her not to do this that they were good together and needed each other. She'd stayed focused on his chin, unable to meet his eyes so he wouldn't guess the truth, but "I'll take care of myself" were the last words she'd said to him. Reminding him of that was the easy way to get some emotional distance in the here and now, but a tiny part of her heart ached at the hurt in his eyes.

"Right. How could I have forgotten?" He gave her a curt nod and left with the medic to go to the infirmary.

She watched him go, letting out a slow breath. Words rose to her tongue, apologies, regrets, but she'd never voice them. Not now. She left the makeshift landing area and walked toward the largest temporary trailer on the site, trying to rein in her emotions. The best thing she could do was focus on her job.

The entire site was set up like a fort from the Old West, which reminded her of Yousef. She hoped he'd taken care of things with the elders and was able to protect his family. She'd always be grateful for the risk he'd taken to be a safe harbor when she needed him most. He was a good man.

Striding into the courtyard of the makeshift fort, she looked around, surprised it seemed deserted. There was no bustle of activity and no one to greet her. That was probably a good thing. If there were a problem, there would be a group of people around moving the trailers out. Since there wasn't a soul in sight, that probably meant they were safe for the moment.

The door slammed shut behind her, and suddenly she was faced with a chair and a door. A voice was coming from the other side of the door, so Brenna took the chair and sat down to wait. The first thing she wanted to say was how sorry she was, but that her cover had been blown the moment Colt had been brought to Saabir's compound. As much as she didn't want to believe it, with their history, and the fact that Colt was about to be tortured, her true identity could have come out.

But was that her only reason? Her conscience still pricked her over the others that had died there. She'd saved Colt, but not them. What did that make her? She'd told herself over and over that the mission had to be top priority, but when it came to Colt, she'd thrown the mission away in a heartbeat. She didn't have to ask herself why. The reason was staring her in the face, she just didn't want to admit it to herself.

She still loved Colt Mitchell.

The thought didn't hit her with the jolt she thought it would. It felt right and good. But there was nothing she could do to act on it. That was the entire reason she'd broken up with him in the first place. Their jobs were dangerous. A relationship between a Special Ops soldier and an intelligence officer would never work. It couldn't. There was too much risk.

She startled when the door behind her opened. Turning, she saw Julian Bennet leaning against the wall dressed in a suit and tie. That wasn't a good sign. It meant he'd flown in from somewhere else for this meeting. She groaned inwardly, but walked over to him, trying not to appear nervous. "Hey, Julian."

He shoved his hands in his pockets, his head lowered as if to gather his thoughts and then faced her head on. "What happened, Brenna? You were our best chance of shutting Nazer down."

"I'm sorry. I'm not going to make excuses, let me say that up front. But he brought in a soldier he'd captured and it happened to be someone I used to know. Captain Colt Mitchell."

At the name, Julian's focus completely changed. He straightened and crossed over to stand in front of her. "You know where Colt Mitchell is?"

Brenna drew her eyebrows down in a frown. "I just sent him to the infirmary to have his injuries looked at. Why? Do you know him?"

"He's here?" Julian pushed past her, but turned before he got to the outer door. "How bad are his injuries?"

She'd never seen Julian like this. He was the most calm and collected man she'd ever met. "Wait. Tell me how you know him?" None of this was making sense.

Julian ran his hands through his hair. "My Special Ops team had intel that Nazer was in northern Afghanistan and during the grab, Colt was captured. We've been trying to track him down for the last three days, but Nazer dropped off the face of the planet."

"Colt works for Griffin Force?" Air whooshed out of her lungs and her knees suddenly didn't seem capable of holding her upright. They were both working for the same task force. "For how long?"

"He came on about the same time you did. I'm just so glad he's alive." Julian didn't seem to realize he'd dropped a bombshell on her. He couldn't keep the happy, relieved smile off his face. Brenna could only stare as she tried to wrap her mind around the fact that she'd been working on the same team as Colt.

We would have crossed paths eventually. Was that fate intervening or coincidence?

"If he went missing three days ago, he must have come immediately to Saabir's compound. No wonder Nazer was with him." Brenna bit her lip, remembering the first time she'd seen Colt, bruised and bleeding. "Saabir was just getting started when we escaped."

Julian put his hands on her shoulders. He knew how hard witnessing the torture had been on her. "Did you get any information on where he's planning his next attack?"

Hope flickered in Julian's eyes. Brenna hated to disappoint him and wished she didn't have to. Capturing terrorists was personal to Julian, but she didn't know why and had never asked. Now didn't seem to be the right time to delve deeper, either.

"No. I had to get Colt out of there before they killed him." She tried to keep her voice level, but could hear the thread of frustration in it, which meant Julian could hear it, too. She had to make him understand she hadn't thrown her undercover post away lightly. "I'm sorry. I'll do anything I can to get another line on him."

"That's next to impossible at this point. The attack is imminent." Julian's hand sliced through the air as he turned away from her. She cringed, but knew she deserved every word. He took a deep breath and faced her. "I'm sorry, that came out harsher than I intended. You did the right thing."

"Thanks." She looked up and met his eyes, seeing the sincerity there. That helped assuage her lingering guilt. "What's our next step?"

The door behind Julian opened and slammed shut again with a tinny clap. They both turned simultaneously to face Colt. He still had on his black cargo pants, but had discarded the *chapan* coat for a clean white t-shirt. He immediately met Brenna's gaze and gave her a nod, but when he settled on Julian, a grin broke out over his face. "I can't tell you how surprised I was to see Elliott in the infirmary. You guys are a sight for sore eyes."

"I bet Elliott was ecstatic. Well, as ecstatic as that guy can get." Julian pulled him in for a side hug, but stopped when Colt winced. "What did he say? How bad is it? You've got a pretty good shiner there."

"Yeah, well, you should see the other guy." Colt smirked.

"I'll bet," Julian said as he carefully squeezed Colt again.

It was strange to see Colt hugging Julian. She didn't know Julian well, but he didn't seem to be the hugging type. Not to mention her professional life and personal life were meeting head on right in front of her eyes. Brenna bit the inside of her cheek. It wasn't ideal, but it didn't scare her like she'd always thought it would.

"Once he washed me off, he was surprised at how well Brenna and our healer did in patching me up. There's nothing that won't heal." He pointed to Brenna, then Julian. "Which brings me to my next question. What's the story here?"

Brenna glanced at Julian. She was still digesting the news they were all working together. How could she explain it to him when she wasn't sure she understood all the angles herself?

He caught her gaze and motioned to the room behind him. "Let's go sit down, Colt. This might take a while."

They walked through the door to a sparse room that had a table and three metal chairs. "Welcome to my office," Julian said with a smile. "The chairs are probably the coolest thing about it. Military chic or something."

Brenna smiled and sat down. In his civilian life, Julian was probably used to the best of everything. She'd bet her service medal he never sat on metal chairs unless he was out in the field. Colt didn't seem to mind, though, and moved his chair next to hers. "You might start a trend with it."

She avoided Colt's gaze, but did a quick sweep of his face before she looked away. His cuts that were visible had been cleaned up. His eye looked better and the little bit of bandage she could see under his collar covered the burn on his neck. She hoped they'd given him something more for the pain. He seemed in good spirits so she was assuming they had.

"Colt, I usually keep certain parts of my organization in Griffin Force separate. My undercover ops don't know what special ops are doing and vice versa. But since you two have previous history, I'm going to fill you in." Julian took a deep breath, as if weighing his words.

Brenna winced inwardly a bit. The way he'd emphasized previous history made her feel defensive somehow, but she'd done nothing wrong. Except walk away from the one man she'd truly loved. She couldn't say that in this room, though, so she stayed silent.

"Brenna had worked closely with some of my British intel buddies and earned herself a reputation as being intuitive and cool under pressure. They mentioned she knew Pashto and had a knack for picking up tough languages." As Julian talked, Brenna felt a flush of pleasure. Those British intel buddies of his hadn't been easy to work with at all, but she'd kept her chin up. Apparently, it hadn't been as bad as she thought, if they'd given her that much praise.

Julian folded his arms and leaned on the table. "I had a situation come up where there was a possibility of getting someone on the inside of Saabir's household and I knew she'd be perfect for the job. With her coloring and knowledge of the language it was meant to be. I approached her about it and she agreed. After some negotiations, she was sold to Saabir as his house slave."

Colt raised his eyebrows and turned his gaze on her. "You were sold as a slave."

His words were a statement, but she saw the question in his eyes. "It sounds a lot worse than it was." Slaves, especially women, were often forced to do other things for ISIS and AQIM fighters. Colt's underlying question was one she'd probably be asked a lot in debriefing. How far had she been pressed?

Thankfully the worst that had happened was feeling the sting of a slap or the rap of a wooden spoon.

Julian put up his hand. "We set everything up with all kinds of contingency plans and you don't have to give her that look. Her safety was paramount."

Brenna nodded to acknowledge the truth of Julian's words. He'd done his best to keep her safe.

"Once Saabir took the bait and Brenna was in, she had several chances to listen while he spoke to Nazer and top tier leadership in AQIM and ISIS. No one cared about the servant girl giving them their meals. From those conversations we were able to get locations on training camps and figure out where the money was coming from. It was the most headway we'd made in shutting Nazer's operation down."

Colt shook his head. "She was the source for our team. We went in on her information. That's how we knew where to strike."

Julian gave him a half-smile. "Yes. So, in a way, you were working together without knowing it."

"And now that source is gone because of me." Colt blew out a breath and stood, his fists clenched as he paced. "You shouldn't have scrubbed the mission, Bren. The scope of this is beyond one man."

She stood as well, anger rushing through her. "What should I have done? Watch them torture you? Listen to you scream until you begged for death? I'd already seen that too many times. How do you think I could live with that memory of you on my conscience?"

Her breaths were ragged and coming fast. She was dealing

with enough guilt of her own. Why was he questioning her now? The room was silent after her outburst and she stepped back. "Sorry," she mumbled. She had to get herself under control. In all her years in the field she'd never had an outburst like that. She was calm, collected and prided herself for being that way. Only Colt Mitchell could bring this out in her. Biting the inside of her lip, she clenched her hands together and took a slow breath in.

Colt reached out and held her forearm until she looked at him. "I'm sorry. I wasn't thinking." The raw emotion in his eyes made the anger melt away. He had always understood her in a way no one else had. Maybe that was still true. He'd been in the field. He knew what it could be like.

Julian broke in, coming around the table to stand next to her and Colt. "I'm sorry, too."

She dropped her gaze and took a moment to gather herself. Her thoughts were all over the place and she didn't like that feeling. Orderly. Planned. That's what she liked. "I'm fine. I did what I had to do."

"And we're grateful for everything you did." Julian leaned forward and put his hand on Colt's shoulder. "You probably didn't know Nazer had sent pictures and a ransom demand for Colt, but we couldn't pinpoint where he was to mount a rescue operation. You accomplished that."

Brenna nodded, not trusting herself to speak. She could only imagine what those pictures of Colt had looked like. Tears were threatening, but she wouldn't allow them to fall. Nazer was evil. He would have killed Colt in a horribly painful way. That's what she couldn't have lived with and that's what she had to remember.

There was a knock at the door, but before Julian could say

come in, the person on the other side opened it. It was a man who was a little on the stocky side. He bypassed everyone else and gave her an appreciative glance before coming to shake her hand. "Hey Brenna. Welcome back."

"Thanks, Augie." He was sweet, like a younger brother, and she smiled at him. He was exactly her eye level, with a shock of red hair that clashed with his bright orange and blue plaid shirt. It wasn't often you saw any plaid that colorful in Afghanistan, but if she needed a wake-up call, just looking at it might do the trick. He was still holding her hand and she gently pulled her fingers back.

Julian cleared his throat, an amused smile on his face. "Augie, did you have something for me?"

He didn't take his eyes off Brenna. "There was a remote tagger on that coat that was brought in."

All humor was sucked out of the room and Brenna's full attention was trained on Augie now. "What do you mean? The coat Colt was wearing?"

"Yeah, it had a tracking device on it. It was dormant, but now it's transmitting. I isolated it in the lab, but whoever is on the other end probably knows where we are." Augie finally looked at Julian, biting his thumbnail. "Sorry."

"Where did you get that coat?" Julian's voice was controlled and while he positioned himself in front of Colt and Brenna, he kept his stance casual. From an outsider's perspective, he might have just asked if the sun was shining. But the question itself put a flare of hopefulness back in Julian's eyes. And she was the one who would fan that flame.

"I grabbed it off Saabir's dining room table right before we escaped. I'd never seen it around the house before so it has to be

Nazer's." Brenna began to pace. Nazer was probably on his way here. He would know they took it.

"So, what you're telling me is we have Nazer's coat and he probably knows where we are and is on his way here right now." Colt shook his head as if he couldn't believe their luck. "You can't make this stuff up."

Augie let his chewed-up thumbnail drop and bit his lip instead. "Well, he probably doesn't care about the coat. He most likely wants the diamonds that were sewn into the sleeves. If I'm guesstimating correctly, there's about $50 million worth in there."

Now it was Julian's turn to look incredulous. "He had diamonds in the coat?" He lifted an arm and patted Augie on the back. "You're amazing."

Brenna watched the exchange, her mind racing. "This is our chance. Those diamonds had to be for financing the attack. If we have them, maybe that will at least delay it, but we have a chance to trap him."

Her words echoed into the room. No one said anything, but they had to be thinking it. "We're bringing him to us. Why not take advantage?" That would also give her a chance to let go of a bit of guilt she was carrying at not finishing the mission she'd been assigned.

Julian grimaced. "It's dangerous because we don't have any time to plan out an op. It might be best to just take the diamonds and get out. It'll cripple his plans and that's better than nothing."

"We can put something together. We've been trying to catch this guy for so long, we have to have a plan that would fit the situation." The more she talked, the more excited she became at the prospect. "We can lure him in, get him in the open, and when he reaches to grab the diamonds, we grab him."

"All right, I'll hear you out. If we're going to even consider this, though, we better get the rest of the team assembled."

Brenna dug her nails into her palm. This was her chance to redeem herself and she was going to take it.

CHAPTER ELEVEN

Colt sat down in the metal chair again, his body begging for some rest. He had to push it a little harder, though. No way was he going to miss this op. It was unlikely that Nazer would come himself to get the coat, but he might—and Colt wanted to be there for his capture. He *had* to be there after all that he'd been through.

Augie was at the computer with Brenna and he watched her lean in, completely focused. She was in her element here, he had to admit that. No wonder Julian had wanted her on the task force. He shook his head. It was unbelievable they'd been working together and hadn't known it. Maybe that was a sign of some sort. But would she see it that way?

The door opened again and Colt wasn't surprised to see Jake Williams and Nate Hughes. The moment he'd seen Elliott, he knew the others couldn't be far away. He stood to hug them, glad for the pills that had dulled the pain so he could lift his arms.

"Thought we'd lost you for good," Jake said gruffly.

"You said you'd be right behind me." Nate gave him a slap on the back and Colt couldn't hold back a grunt of pain. "Sorry, man. What happened?"

Colt could feel Brenna's eyes on them, but he didn't look her way. "I was thrown out a window and the next thing I knew I was being dragged into some shack for questioning. How's your leg?"

Nate waved off his question. "Through and through. Lots of blood, but no permanent damage. Even if it had been more serious I wouldn't have noticed it. All we could think about was finding you."

"Those pictures . . ." Jake's voice trailed off, a pained expression on his face. "I'm just glad you're back."

Colt nodded. "Nazer wanted to bait you. The guy's got some serious issues with Griffin Force."

"Yeah, well, he's pretty high on my put-the-guy-away list." Jake sat down in the chair next to Colt's. "I heard we've got a plan in place."

"There was a tracker on us when we got here. It was dormant, that's why it didn't set off any alarms right away, but it activated about fifteen minutes ago." He motioned toward Brenna. "She thought it was the perfect opportunity to grab whoever comes to get it."

"Do you think Nazer would risk it?" Nate asked, turning the last chair around and sitting in it backwards.

"Maybe. I hope so." Colt gingerly folded his arms. "This is going to go down fast and dirty."

"And you're not up for it." Julian walked over to stand behind him. "You're injured and need to be evacuated. We're pulling up stakes and transport is getting ready to leave. You need to be with them."

Colt twisted his body to see the man behind him. "I'm not missing this. I'm fine."

"You'll follow orders." Julian's voice was firm. There wouldn't be any arguing with him when he used that tone. If it was any other day, any other situation, Colt would let it go, but he couldn't.

When Julian turned to walk away, Colt reached out and grabbed his forearm. "I nearly died because of this guy. Don't sideline me. Not now."

Julian stared him down and Colt met his gaze without flinching. "Okay, but you stay in the tech room with Augie. You don't go anywhere except that room, got it? We can't afford to put you in the field in your condition."

"Deal." A tech room wasn't exactly where Colt wanted to be, but at least he wouldn't be with the exit team having Elliott fuss over his wounds.

Julian turned to Brenna and Augie. "Everything in place?"

Brenna nodded. "The coat is being loaded up as we speak. The convoy will be three trucks, four people per truck. We're going to go grab what we need, then we'll get everyone in place."

"It has to look real or they'll know something's up." Julian pointed out.

Confident and professional Brenna was definitely in place as she spoke. "It'll look real. We'll give them a good show, stay safe, and grab who we can. With as little notice as they had, they're probably flying as blind as we are." She headed for the door. "Let's get going, Augie. I'll help you supervise the tech equipment being moved to transport."

"Yes, ma'am." He hurried after her and Colt felt a twinge of regret that he wasn't her partner this time. He'd sort of gotten used to being with her. It was odd how quickly that comfortable feeling had come back. The sadness and anger that he'd associated with their relationship had vanished during their escape, replaced with a need to be with her. All that was left was uncertainty about how she was feeling. As soon as this was over, he wanted to sit down and talk it out with her. Or at least find some closure if she still wanted to walk away. At least now that they were on the same team, it was a bit easier to find her.

"Well, you heard her, boys. We need to go tac up and remember, make it look good, but safety is our first priority." Julian followed after Brenna and Augie. "We've probably only got another fifteen to get the site broken down and everything ready for those trucks, so let's move."

Jake waited for Colt to stand up. "You sure you're up for this? You've been through a lot."

"I wouldn't miss it. Besides, I'll just be in the tech room." Colt tried not to let any disappointment show through in his voice. He wanted to be out with his team, but Julian was right. He wasn't up for it right now.

Jake kept pace with him as they followed Julian down the hall. "I'm sorry about what happened," he said finally. "I know Nazer was probably using you to get to me. To all of us."

"Don't feel guilty. You told me to evacuate and I didn't. The responsibility's on me." Colt put a hand to his side. His deep cut would leave a scar big enough that he wouldn't forget his mission here for the rest of his life. "I'm just grateful Brenna was in a position to help me escape." And not a moment too soon. The memory of the sadistic look in Saabir's eyes was going to haunt him for a long time to come.

"We all are." Jake's gaze followed his and landed on Brenna and Augie at the end of the hall. "From the very little I know about her, she's a good agent. Going undercover at Saabir's had to be difficult, though."

He thought back to the few things she'd mentioned that she'd witnessed while there. "Yeah. She's amazing. I knew her when we were both fresh out of the academy."

Jake slowed a bit as they neared Brenna. "You've got a history with her then?"

Colt shrugged, trying to keep it casual, but the smile on his face told a different story. "You could say that."

"Be careful then, man. Emotions getting tangled up on a mission can be deadly."

"Speaking from experience?" Colt raised an eyebrow, unable to resist a little dig in Jake's direction. "How's Mya?"

Jake had met Mya on their last mission and they'd been nearly inseparable ever since. The thought made him pause. If he was to get a second chance with Brenna, Jake might have some advice on how to be in a relationship when you worked together. He scrubbed a hand over his face. That was definitely putting the cart before the horse.

"You know, Mya's barely slept the last three days trying to make contact with anyone who might have a line on you. We were worried." Jake stepped up to join Brenna and Augie who were waiting for them. "She was pretty relieved when I told her you'd been found."

"Tell her thanks," Colt said. He'd always liked Mya. She had a big heart. Like Brenna. He wouldn't think that would make them ideal candidates for this kind of work, but they were good at it. Their compassion gave them an edge when it came to reading people.

Augie was back to chewing on his thumbnail. "Mya and her father have a lot of contacts in several governments. They even talked to reclusive rebels most spy agencies can't even find. It's astonishing, really. I was trying to peek through their notes of who they'd already spoken with and couldn't believe it when I saw they'd talked to the Wazir tribal leaders. They're fairly reclusive, you know, and their Maliks don't talk to just anyone."

Julian gave him a patient smile. "I had no idea. And just to be clear, I'd never play you in any trivia game, Augie."

Colt noticed he didn't talk down to Augie, but his tone was less gruff than it was when he talked to the rest of the team members. "So, is everything in place?"

Augie stared at him for a moment before snapping back to the conversation at hand. "Yes. The coat is in the second truck in a metal briefcase. The tracker is transmitting. We're good to go."

Julian turned to the rest of the assembled team. "The three trucks will lead Nazer's team away from us and we'll finish breaking down the site and moving out. Our main objective is to lure Nazer's team in and take as many prisoners as we can. Alive. So put on a show of force, but stay safe."

Brenna pointed to the door behind them. "We'll have Jake lead the team in the first truck, Nate in the second and I'll be in the third."

"Where are you going to be, Augie?" Colt asked.

"We'll be watching the security footage here." He pointed

toward a small trailer in the corner of the "fort." "Only until the op is over and we'll move out with the rest."

Which was exactly what Colt didn't want, but one look at Julian's face and he knew he wasn't going to bring it up again. "Great. I can help keep an eye on things."

"Exactly." Augie gave Colt a big smile, completely missing the sarcasm. Colt felt guilty. It was easy to see Augie was sincere and a little awkward, but very good at his job and he didn't want to make the guy uncomfortable.

"If we're breaking down this site, where will you take the prisoners?" Colt turned to Julian.

"I have that covered." he answered brusquely, totally in mission mode. "Let's get in position."

Colt needed to sit down again, but there was no way he was going to show any weakness in front of these guys. "Show me the way to the tech room, Augie."

He moved down the hall, but Colt stopped to watch Julian hand Brenna a pistol as she shifted to put her body armor on. So many conflicting emotions were rushing through him—fierce pride at seeing her doing the things they'd trained for and cold fear that something would happen to her.

"Be careful," Colt said, just loud enough for her to hear. He'd surprised himself by speaking his thoughts out loud, but he couldn't think about the distance between them becoming a permanent one.

She looked up, surprise in her eyes. "I will."

With her armor on and a pistol in her hand, she was ready for battle. But experience had taught him that so many things could go wrong. Unease shot up his spine. This was a thrown together op, they needed more time to think things through.

Yet it was their best shot. Part of him wanted to say something more to Brenna as an uneasy feeling washed over him again, but what could he say? I want to pick up where we left off? Not the time. "See you on the other side."

She nodded and walked away. He watched her go, wanting to call her back. Again. When would he quit watching her walk away and do something about it?

He followed Augie down the hall to a room on the far side of the building. The moment they were in and the door secured, he slumped down in the nearest chair. He rubbed his fingers over the bridge of his nose, fighting the urge for sleep. At least the cheek and eye swelling had gone down so he could see clearly now. If he could stay awake, that is.

"You look like you could use some coffee." Augie walked to the corner of the small room and took out a mug. "I keep some in here for the all-nighters." He poured the black brew into the mug and sat down next to Colt. "You have feelings for Agent Wilson, don't you?"

Colt had taken a small sip and nearly spit out the liquid that Augie was passing off as coffee. "What do you mean?"

"I could tell back there." He leaned closer. "She doesn't date soldiers. Or anyone who works on the team. Lots of the guys have tried, but she shuts them all down." He gave Colt a sympathetic look. "Just a heads up so you don't waste your time."

Colt wasn't sure what to respond to first. It wasn't a big shock that Brenna had a no dating in the workplace rule. Fraternization wasn't a problem unless one person was a superior over the other, but Brenna wasn't taking chances with anyone in the profession from the sounds of it. Would her rule stand if he tried again?

It didn't surprise him that other men on the team had tried to be with her. She was beautiful, smart, and capable. What guy wouldn't want that? But he wasn't about to admit any feelings he may or may not have for her to Augie. "Thanks for the tip, man." Hopefully that would shut down this line of conversation.

Augie turned to the monitors in the corner. The trucks weren't even five miles away from the site, yet. "Looks like they've got company. Nazer's men are coming up fast, right behind our decoy." He put on a headset. "The targets are on the move."

A shot of adrenaline bolted through Colt. He watched as Nazer's two vehicles drew closer, men with guns hanging out the window. What were they thinking? They were outmanned and outgunned. Were the diamonds really worth their lives? That's when he saw the little bits of dust and dirt kicking up all along the side and back of the convoy.

Those were shots coming from above.

A helo flew into view just as the third truck exploded in a fiery ball of flame. Colt stood, his gaze riveted to the burning truck, everything suddenly in slow motion. That was Brenna's truck. Was there any way she had survived?

Please don't let her be dead.

There was chaos on the ground as the helo came back for round two and Nazer's trucks overtook the rest of the convoy. Gunfire had erupted and Colt could only watch helplessly as the team fended off the attack. "Do we have any air support?" he asked Augie, his voice urgent. "They need something."

This was all wrong. He wasn't supposed to be here watching. He was supposed to be out there with them. Jake was calling a retreat for everyone to fall back to the lead truck. The men ran for it. *Come on, come on,* Colt murmured as they made it one by one.

Just as the last one reached the lead truck, Colt saw one of Nazer's men rushing toward the middle vehicle, the flash of the metal briefcase holding the coat in his hand. They'd taken the bait. Would they take what they came for and leave now?

The helo's strafing kept Jake and his team's heads down, their vehicles left with nothing but flat tires while Nazer's two trucks trundled away. It was over. Colt practically fell into his seat. "They took it and we've got a line on them. How many prisoners did we get? Can you see anything?"

Augie didn't answer, just kept tapping away at his keyboard. Colt's eyes were riveted to the screen. When the smoke finally cleared, there was one man kneeling on the ground, his hands behind his head. The surveillance zoomed in on his face and Colt stood. That was a face Colt would never forget. Saabir. They'd gotten him. Colt couldn't help the frisson of gladness running through him. If they couldn't have Nazer, his right hand man was the second best thing.

Any pleasure he felt at Saabir's capture was short-lived, though, as he watched Jake and his men comb the truck wreckage. Where was Brenna? He didn't see her on the feed at all and it was confirmed when Jake Williams' voice came over the headset. "Augie, we're missing a man."

Augie's brow furrowed. "Did you find . . ." he swallowed and found his voice. "A body?"

"No. You need to go over the security feeds and see what happened. And turn on our own tracker on that *chapan.*"

Augie began typing furiously on his laptop. "That helo came

out of nowhere. We didn't even know Nazer had access to one."
He was murmuring to himself, but saying what Colt was thinking. Would it have made a difference in the op decisions if they
had known? Maybe.

"There, there she is," Augie said, pointing to the monitor.
"That first truck picked Agent Wilson up."

Colt's entire body went cold at Augie's words. "What do you
mean?"

The images on the monitor didn't lie. Brenna was being
carried fireman-style and thrust into the back of a truck. Colt
clenched his fist. She wasn't moving. His heart fell like a lead
ball smashing through everything vital to living. Was she dead
or just unconscious?

But the monitor couldn't show them anything more. It was
too late. They'd taken her.

CHAPTER TWELVE

B renna tried to clear her head, the pain and nausea
making everything muddled. Her ears were ringing
from the truck exploding. She'd barely had time from
the moment she heard the whine of the missile to shout to the
other three men to jump before she jumped herself. The explosion had pushed her clear of the fireball, but she'd been
knocked unconscious. When she came to, she was in the back
of the truck, her hands tied behind her back. How had this
happened? Where had Nazer gotten a helicopter?

She tried to move, but it was nearly impossible with the
numbness in her hands and arms. If the pain in her shoulders
was any indication, she'd been tied up in the back of this truck
for hours. Dust was choking her the more they bumped over
the road and she wished she had her hijab with her to protect
her from it. As it was, all she could do was try to burrow her
face into her collar to breathe.

Willing her mind to think of anything else, she focused on

Colt. The look on his face when he'd told her to be careful had been so charged with emotion it cracked wide open that box of feelings she'd buried. For so long her heart had been closed to any feelings beyond getting the job done that it shocked her to feel torn about something. She didn't know how to react, so she'd practically run away to this op.

Regrets were piling up fast and furious wherever Colt was concerned, but that one topped them all. There was no doubt in her mind that Nazer was going to kill her and she wouldn't have a chance to make anything right.

She squirmed, pulling at her bonds, but only succeeded in hurting her shoulder again. The truck ride was going on forever, but the reality was, it was preferable to what was coming next. It did look like they were traveling away from the mountains, though, so maybe they were going back to the hideout she knew. If they were, there would be a small chance of escape.

After at least ten potholes and one swerve, the truck finally stopped. Brenna tensed. The back flap of the truck pulled back and a man she'd never seen before loomed in the space. "*Derdzem.*" He motioned her with his hand to come toward him.

She looked away. How did he expect her to move when she was trussed up like a Christmas goose? He made a low growl in his throat and climbed in the back, yanking her up by the arm. She couldn't help the cry of pain. Her shoulder joints were so taut they felt like they were being stabbed with glass shards.

He threw her out of the back of the truck and she hit the ground hard with no way to use her hands. Her body armor cushioned the fall somewhat, but tears pricked her eyes at the pain. *Do not cry*, she willed herself. Anger boiled within her and she fed that emotion.

The man picked her up by the arm again and dragged her to a mud hut. She did her best to try and get the lay of the land, but it looked like they were in the middle of nowhere. Dirt and sagebrush as far as the eye could see. Was this some sort of look out? The hut didn't have an actual door, just an open doorway. He pulled her through it and dumped her unceremoniously on the floor. She scrambled to a sitting position and made herself as small as possible. Adrenaline shot through her as she thought about how isolated the two of them were.

He didn't approach her, however, just squatted in front of the doorway. They stared at each other for what seemed like an eternity, but she broke the eye contact when she heard the roar of another vehicle. Ah, so this was just the delivery point, a way station.

Her stomach clenched, knowing it had to be Nazer in that car coming to get her. Her captor turned and stood, leaving his perch. He offered greetings to whomever was just out of her sight line. It wasn't long, though, before Nazer's shadow was in the doorway. She looked up at him, surprised that he had a small bandage across the bridge of his nose and the area around his eyes was bruised. It gave her a little burst of satisfaction that Colt had done that.

"*Ghla,*" he murmured. He hadn't shaved for a while and his dark beard added more shadows to his angular face, giving it an air of malevolence.

Brenna kept her face blank, trying to calm her racing heart, but fear arrowed through her. He was calling her a thief, which, from his perspective of having his *chapan* taken, was true. She kept her face raised, looking into his eyes. She'd had enough of staring at the floor when it came to these people. If this was the end, she was going to look them in the eye.

He approached her and grabbed her hair, pulling her up. Tears gathered at the pain in her scalp and she scrambled to her feet as best she could. He undid the bindings on her hands and started undoing the Velcro straps on her body armor. She flinched away, but he slapped her face. "Hold still," he commanded in English. "Or I'll kill you now."

As opposed to later? His words chilled her, confirming what she already knew. He was definitely going to kill her.

"Who are you?" He dropped her vest to the ground, looking over her clothing with a derisive sneer. "How long have you been spying for the Americans?"

She stared up into his coal black eyes, a chill running through her at the vacant, callous look of him. She'd watched him order people to be killed, and it was obvious he'd lost his soul long ago. "I don't know what you're talking about."

He slapped her face again and she covered her stinging cheek. "You worked in Saabir's household for months, lawfully sold to him as a former slave to the loyal fighters. You betrayed me with your lies."

She was silent. What could she say to that?

He circled her and she resisted the urge to turn and keep him in her sight at all times. When he came around to the front again, she lifted her chin.

"What is your name? Your real name?" His voice was quiet now and that made his question sound so much more sinister.

"You said it earlier. *Ghla*. Thief. That's who I am." Her voice sounded a little high-pitched, but she kept it even. Dignified. She was proud of that in the face of his evilness.

He moved into her space until her nose nearly touched his shoulder. "You will regret everything you ever stole from me." He turned to the man who'd brought her in and spoke in rapid Pashto. "Where is the *chapan*? Did you check it for tracking devices like I instructed?"

The man who'd brought her stood. "*Hao*. I did find one, but the explosion must have disabled it. No one followed us." He rose and went to the truck to retrieve the coat.

Brenna listened carefully to their conversation and swallowed back her frustration. Maybe he was wrong. Maybe Colt could still find her and the tracker was just dormant or something. She needed to sit tight and keep her head.

The man returned and Nazer nearly snatched the coat from him. Pulling a razor blade out, he began slitting the sleeves of the garment. Diamonds fell at his feet and he smiled. "They didn't find them." He bent to look at them, picking up a large one. His eyes narrowed in suspicion. "No." He picked up a few more. "There weren't any this size." His attention flicked to Brenna. "Did you know about the diamonds?"

She pursed her lips.

He took one step toward her and held the razor blade to her neck. The point dug into her skin. "Answer me now or die right here."

A tiny drop of blood seeped out and trickled down her neck. She gasped. "No. I didn't know."

"Liar." He went outside and when he came back in he had a jeweler's loupe. He examined several of the diamonds. His face twisted with anger. "These are all fake." He paced the room and

Brenna braced herself, knowing she would take the brunt of whatever he was feeling.

"Let's tie up the loose ends. Destroy this immediately." He held out the *chapan* to the other man. "Build a fire."

The man immediately complied, using the fire pit right outside the door to get a small flame going. Brenna sat down and watched with dismay as her long-shot chance of the tracker still giving off a signal went up in smoke.

Her mind was so caught up in the crackle of the *chapan* burning that she didn't hear the whine of the small plane engine until it was nearly overhead. "Get up," Nazer ordered her.

She stood. No use causing herself any more unnecessary pain.

He was in her face again, his eyes flashing. "I will find out exactly who you are and make you suffer before you die." He looked down at her vest on the floor, his face twisting as if he hated the sight of it. "I have plans and since I had to sacrifice Saabir, you will take his place."

Her eyebrows came together in confusion. How could she take Saabir's place? He was Nazer's go-to man for torturing people. She could never do that.

Since she couldn't voice her questions, she kept quiet. Nazer took her arm and pushed her out of the little hut. The sunlight was blinding, even though she had only been inside the dark little hut for an hour or so. Nazer and his man flanked her on either side as they stalked toward the plane. She hadn't realized that the isolation of the hut was more because they needed the room for a small airstrip. There were so many angles to consider when it came to Nazer and his operation, but right now, all she could think about was what he had planned for her.

None of it would be good.

Brenna looked to the sky. If the team had any idea of where she was, now would be the time to make their presence known. But no help came and she was strapped into the plane's seat. Pressing back, the plane's engines roared to life and before long they were airborne.

Part of her wanted to look back. To say her goodbyes if only in her mind, but that would mean she'd given up and that wasn't something she could do. She would fight until the end.

With her resolve in place she faced forward, ready for whatever was coming.

CHAPTER THIRTEEN

Colt pressed his fingers into his eyes. "There's got to be someone else we can contact, Mya. Anyone."

"We're doing our best, just let me do my job. Why don't you go rest or something? You look exhausted." Mya twisted away from her laptop to give him a pointed look.

He was. But how could he sleep when Brenna was Nazer's prisoner? The longer she was with him, the less chance she had of being found alive. His heart squeezed at the thought. "I'll rest when we find her." How had they lost the signal in that coat? Why hadn't he insisted he be on the op with her? Maybe he could have saved her.

Julian put a hand on his shoulder. "Actually, I'm ordering you to the cot in the next room. If we find out anything, I'll come and get you, but you're no good to her in this condition."

Colt knew he couldn't say no to a direct order, but at this point he was past caring. He had one more item of business before he did anything else. "Who's questioning Saabir?"

Julian didn't look surprised at the question. "Jake."

"Do you think that's a good idea considering all the history he has with Nazer?" Colt clenched his fist, the memory flashing through his mind of his own beating meted out by Saabir while he lay strapped to a metal cot.

"Jake's got a lot of experience with interrogation." Julian motioned toward the door with his head. "Get some rest."

Colt stood. "Let me try to get Nazer's location out of Saabir. I know I can do it." His hand involuntarily went to his right side, which had taken the biggest pounding. "Saabir and I got to know each other in the last few days."

"Which is exactly why I don't want you anywhere near him. It's too personal."

"That's why I'm the perfect person. I escaped. He's got to hate that. Let me try. What harm can it do?"

Julian puffed out a breath. "Okay, I'll give you some time with him, but Jake has to be in there with you. Nothing gets out of hand."

"Fine by me." Colt stood slowly. "Where is he?"

"The other end of the building."

Colt nodded. "Just out of curiosity, how many black sites do you have in operation?"

"I'd have to sit down and count." Julian smiled, but he looked as tired as Colt felt. "Don't worry. We've got what we need to take these guys down."

"What made you go into this business? It seems so personal for you." Colt's fear for Brenna was his constant reminder of why this was personal for him.

Julian shook his head. "I'll tell you another time. Saabir's waiting." He turned to talk to Mya, effectively shutting down the conversation with Colt. Had he touched a nerve?

Colt walked down the hall, his mind going over what had just happened. He didn't know Julian well, but there was something about the guy. He was driven, that's for sure. Whatever the reason for Griffin Force, Colt was grateful for it. Government task forces were subject to all kinds of oversight and red tape. Finding Brenna would be nearly impossible, but Griffin Force could take intel and use it right away. They were her only chance.

Focusing on questioning Saabir, he clenched and unclenched his fists. He had to be in control, but that was going to be difficult. He needed Brenna back. That had to be his mantra and first priority. But he also wanted a little revenge and that's where he could get into trouble.

Opening the door, he wasn't surprised to see Saabir shackled to a chair. Jake was standing over him, and raised a brow when Colt entered. "Hey. What's going on?"

"Just came to catch up with my old friend." Colt slowly closed the door behind him. "How are things going?"

"Great. He was just telling me how much he hates Western-ers." Jake moved aside to lean against the wall, like they had all the time in the world.

"It must gall him that he had one working in his household and didn't even know it." Colt moved toward Saabir, but kept his eyes on Jake.

"She was a deceiver like every other Westerner. And she'll pay for her crimes." Saabir smiled. "Maybe Nazer will send you a picture of her dead and broken body."

Colt's fist connected to his jaw before he could take another breath or say anything else about Brenna. Even the thought of her dead fueled rage inside his body. The fact was, though, she could be dead already. He couldn't let himself go there. He had to stay focused on getting information out of Saabir.

He spit on the ground, his lip bloodied. "She'll get what she deserves."

Colt flexed his hand without taking his eyes off Saabir. The guy was talking about Brenna in the present tense. Not "she got what she deserved", but she'll get it. That was a sliver of hope.

"What does she deserve?" Jake asked, moving between the two men.

Saabir just leaned his head back and didn't say anything. Jake refused to let that stand and forced his face forward. "Tell us where Nazer is going."

When he didn't respond, Colt stepped forward. So many feelings were rushing through him, but anger and anxiety were at the forefront. "He loves to use drug cocktails. Maybe we should see how he likes that sort of thing. Do we have any interrogation enhancers?"

"Sadly no." Jake stepped back. "What else is he fond of?"

"Water boarding." Just saying the words left a bad taste in his mouth, but he saw a flash of fear cross Saabir's face before he could hide it.

Jake raised his eyes to Colt, concern in them. "He water-boarded you?"

"I was coming off the drugs he'd given me and he thought that would speed up the process." He still remembered the fear shooting through his veins when the cloth had been put over his face. If Saabir was scared, they could use that fear to get information, but would that be crossing a line?

He motioned for Jake to walk to the corner near the door. Colt spoke softly. "He's afraid of waterboarding, I can see it in his face. We have to use that."

Jake shook his head. "You know we can't stoop to their level."

"We can bluff. Play with his mind a little." He looked back at Saabir. Colt didn't want to be anywhere near his level, either.

Jake squinted and looked at the ceiling, contemplating his answer. He finally nodded. "I'll go get the water."

He opened the door and stepped out. Colt turned to face Saabir. "Looks like I get to finish what you started in that little hut behind your house. Only you'll be on the receiving end."

Saabir straightened in his chair. "It doesn't matter what you do. I won't tell you where Nazer is. Or the woman."

Colt would bet Nazer wouldn't let Brenna out of his sight. If he found one of them, he'd find the other. "I just want you to know what it feels like."

Saabir shook his head, his eyes bleak. "You think I don't know? I've been a soldier a long time. I've seen it all. Done it all."

He probably had done it all, but he hadn't experienced it all. From the reports on him, Saabir had tortured and killed at least a dozen people, but there wasn't any records on him ever being a prisoner. Maybe that's why he was afraid of the water boarding because he'd dished it out, knew it was excruciating, but hadn't been on the receiving end of it.

"We don't have to do it. No one has to get hurt. Just tell us what we want to know."

Saabir's eyes narrowed. "I won't help you. No matter what." The bleakness had been replaced with a grim frown.

Jake returned with a pail of water and a face cloth. "Ready." He stood in front of their prisoner. "Are you sure this is the route you want to go?"

Saabir pulled on his restraints, the shackles clanking against the chair. "Well, you could try some of the other techniques your coalition countries enjoy inflicting. Play some of your horrific rock music for days. Refuse me food and sleep. Why jump right to water boarding?" He was mocking them now.

"We're on a tight schedule." Colt pulled Saabir's head back, the cloth in his other hand. "For the last time, tell me where Nazer is."

Real fear flashed in Saabir's eyes, but he remained silent. Colt put the cloth over Saabir's face. "Last chance."

Jake deliberately sloshed some of the water on Saabir's pants and he flinched, instinctively turning his face away. Colt held it in place. Flashbacks to being in Saabir's exact position not long ago was making his stomach roil now their roles were reversed. *Please break. Don't make me do this.*

He was desperate to save Brenna, but in this instant, he knew he couldn't actually waterboard someone. This bluff had to be the best acting job Colt had ever done. He bent over and took a deep breath before he let a drop of water fall onto the cloth, watching it dribble down Saabir's chin. He tipped the pail and let another sprinkle of water fall on his chin just below the cloth.

The man was practically hyperventilating. He pulled at his restraints. "Okay, okay, I'll tell you." Colt ripped the cloth away so Saabir could talk. "He's going to Syria."

Colt's blood ran cold. If Nazer had taken Brenna to Syria,

death would be better than what she'd face as a westerner with ISIS soldiers. "How?"

"By plane. He has a private airstrip. About fifteen miles from where we caught up with the *chapan*."

Holding the cloth above Saabir's face as if he might use it again, he looked into the man's eyes. It was hard to tell if he was being truthful, but in case he was, Colt had to get to that airstrip and verify this story for himself. If he was lucky, she'd still be there and he could head them off before they left Afghanistan.

Colt threw the cloth in the bucket. "I'll get things ready to go."

Saabir laughed. "He's gone by now. You'll never catch him once he's in Syria."

"If I don't find him, I'll come back for you and make sure you get thrown into the darkest prison I can find where you'll never see daylight again." Colt pointed a finger at him. "And that's a promise."

Augie rushed into the room, holding up Saabir's phone. "I hacked into it."

From the grin on his face, Colt knew that Augie had more good news. "And?"

"It's a gold mine." Augie was fairly bursting with nervous energy as he went up on the balls of his feet. "Everything we've been looking for."

The band of frustration that had been crushing Colt's ribs since realizing Brenna was gone loosened a little. "Anything about where Nazer took her?"

Augie nodded. "Oh yeah. I know exactly where they are."

"Saabir just told us they were in Syria." He moved to brush

by Augie, but felt a tug on his sleeve. There was no way to shake the guy off without being rude, so he waited.

"She's not in Syria," Augie said quietly.

Colt's gaze shot to Saabir, who'd gone absolutely still. They'd nearly waterboarded him and he'd still lied. "Then where?" There weren't many places worse than Syria, but Colt could think of a few. He watched Augie's mouth, not wanting to hear those places come out of it.

"Let's take this outside." Jake held the door as they walked into the hall. "Okay, Augie, what have you got?"

"I traced a lot of calls to Chris Cornell." Augie looked around expectantly as if the name should ring a bell for them.

Colt fairly growled with frustration. "Just tell me where she is."

Jake held up a hand. "Wait. So Saabir is calling a known British drug trafficker? Cornell is wanted by every international law enforcement agency there is for his crimes. What does that have to do with Brenna?"

Cornell. As soon as Jake had mentioned Britain, everything had clicked. The guy was the worst kind of scum imaginable. "Last I heard, he expanded his business to include human trafficking," Colt said grimly. Not that it surprised him Nazer's group was in business with him. *Low-lifes attract other low-lifes.* "He's using Cornell's trafficking routes to smuggle her into another country isn't he?"

"I traced the number to Britain, and one of the voicemails talked about how they have forty gallons of acetone and ten gallons of hydrogen peroxide ready and waiting."

"TATP. In Britain." Colt's mind was racing. Everything was starting to make sense. "The Canadian Parliament buildings

were a test run. They're going to attack the British Parliament."
He yanked open the door. That was it. They'd figured it out.
And after everything Brenna had sacrificed to find out where
the next attack would be, she wasn't here with the task force to
follow through. It wasn't right.

"Great work, Augie," Jake praised. "I'll let Julian know we've
got a location for Nazer and hopefully for Brenna as well. Get
ready to move out."

Colt nodded, remembering Nazer hiding behind a woman
while the building burned. The man would use anyone to save
himself and somehow Colt knew he'd use Brenna in the attack
he'd planned. It would be something he'd get a sick pleasure out
of— using a woman who'd betrayed him and his organization
to help destroy a target. It was a bonus she was a Westerner as
well.

But Colt was coming to get her. If it was the last thing he
did, he would find her.

"Hold on, Bren." He said it out loud, putting the words into
the universe. Somehow, deep down in her subconscious, in the
history of what they'd shared and what they'd meant to each
other, he hoped she knew that he wouldn't give up on her. "I'm
going to bring you home."

CHAPTER FOURTEEN

Brenna awoke to cold air blowing in her face and the feeling of barbed wire being wrapped around her head and pounded into her brain. She'd never had a worse headache. After the helicopter had landed at another airstrip, Nazer had held her down and injected her with something that felt like death and darkness. Now that she was finally coming to, her body was protesting.

"Where am I?" she managed to croak. Wheels clacked underneath her and she was moving fairly quickly over uneven ground. Was this a gurney? She cracked open an eye and saw a man dressed as a paramedic above her.

"Just lie still, ma'am, we're almost to the hospital." The paramedic's accent sounded British, but that didn't mean she was in the country. The overcast skies and lack of suffocating heat might mean she was in Britain, though. It had been so long since she'd felt anything but the scorching hot weather of Afghanistan.

Twisting a little more, she could see a fully armed guard right behind the paramedic. He was looking straight ahead and she followed his gaze to the multi-storied building they were approaching. The paramedic's words finally penetrated the fog of her thoughts. "Hospital? What's happened?" She pulled on her wrist that was shackled to the metal safety bar on the gurney. What was going on?

"Your doctor will be with you shortly to explain everything." They rattled through some automatic doors and she could smell the antiseptic assaulting her senses.

"Please, tell me what hospital I'm at." Brenna needed to know that she wasn't in Afghanistan anymore as well as exactly where Nazer had taken her. "And why do I have handcuffs on?"

"You're at St. Andrews hospital, in London, ma'am," the paramedic told her. "Here we are."

He parked her gurney in a private room while the guard took up a sentry position right outside her door. "Your nurse will be in shortly," the paramedic said before he checked her safety rails and drew the curtain behind him.

She was finally alone.

London. The Parliament buildings. It all made sense now. But one thing wasn't clear. Nazer said he was going to use her in his plan, but why handcuff her and put her in the hospital?

Brenna tried to sit up, but the room spun crazily and she nearly fell off the gurney. The handcuffs bit into her wrist and she held back a gasp of pain. Lying back down, she held her head with her free hand. How could she get word out?

Before any sort of plan could form, the door opened and her curtain was drawn back. Nazer stood in front of her, dressed in a doctor's white coat with dress pants, a white shirt and tie. It was strange to see him dressed like any other westerner. "I'm surprised to see you awake considering the amount of drugs I gave you." He moved to the side of the gurney and she held herself still. Fear tingled up her spine at how helpless she was lying there in handcuffs. He held all the cards right now and she didn't want to cash in her chips by provoking him. "It would have been easier if you'd slept longer, but now we can move everything forward a bit."

Brenna was surprised at how talkative he seemed. Maybe she could get something out of him. Trying to clear the mental haze in her brain, she focused on his face. "What do you mean?"

"You're about to fulfill a vital part of my plan." He looked back toward the door, as if making sure no one could overhear. "You give us a reason to be here, but don't worry, it won't be for long. You'll be transported as soon as we have what we need. The hospital doesn't want a convicted murderer in their hospital, but I've assured them you're headed to Broadmoor, the place where all of the criminally insane belong."

Brenna furrowed her brow and tried to order her jumbled thoughts. Whatever drug he'd given her had scrambled her brain. It was as if she couldn't process what her senses were telling her. "I don't understand. A murderer?" She closed her eyes. Trying to dig deep into her mental reserves she opened her eyes again. She couldn't give in now.

His smirk broadcasted the fact that he found the situation funny. "It's brilliant, really. You're under guard as a convicted killer."

"Someone is going to figure this out." They had to. There

were worldwide bulletins out for Nazer. Surely someone would recognize him and alert the police.

"No one will think to look twice at a respected doctor helping you get where you belong." He patted the handcuff. "And there's no way to escape so don't even think of it. All you have to do is lie here quietly until I come to collect you."

Yeah, right. Even in her muddled state, she knew that wasn't going to happen. The moment he left she would be planning to escape somehow.

"I can hear the wheels turning in your mind," Nazer said with an annoying cluck of his tongue. "And just to ensure you will do what I say, I've taken precautions."

She clenched her jaw, rage flowing through her. There wasn't anyone in the world she despised more than Nazer al-Raimi.

He held a stack of pictures close to her face. "This is your brother, John, currently on deployment with the Canadian Armed Forces in the Ukraine." He showed her the next one, going quickly through the pile. "This is John with his team, and here's one of him at his barracks, getting his morning coffee." He was methodical. "I have a man on him at all times. If you betray me at any time or refuse to do what I ask, the kill order will be given, and John will be dead before you know to beg for his life."

Brenna blinked, reeling with shock. Her entire body was frozen, as if he'd poured ice over her, numbing her physically, but pushing her to every emotional limit. How could he have found John? She stared at the pictures of the brother she hadn't seen in nearly two years, since his deployment. Tears stung the back of her throat, but she swallowed them back. This was a scare tactic, and it was working. "I don't have a brother."

Nazer chuckled. "I know everything about you, Brenna Wilson. I know your history, your family, your secrets." He reached out and put his hand on her forehead. Anyone looking in would think he was a caring doctor, checking for a fever, but the force of his hand pinned her to the bed, and his fingers dug into her skull. He bent down until his face was all she could see. "I own you."

She pushed back, whipping her head out from under his hand. If only she could head butt the guy, but pain was already crashing through her brain at the slightest movement and the dark edges of unconsciousness were creeping in. She fought to stay alert. "You don't own me. You never will."

Nazer took his hand away, but stared at her, his black eyes filled with contempt. "Make no mistake, you will die. The only question is whether your brother will die, too." He turned on his heel and went to the door where he paused. "There's no turning back now. Everything is in motion and can't be stopped." And then he was gone.

Brenna sank back onto her pillow. She had to get word out to someone. Anyone. She was the only one who could stop him, and she wouldn't fail this time. Glancing around the room she didn't see anything useful to her. It was stripped bare. There was only a set of drawers on the far side. She took a deep breath and sat up again. The dizziness was still there, but she grasped the safety handles. Too much was at stake for her to be lying down, shackled or not.

She put her feet on the floor and pushed off. Once she was

standing on her own two feet, she tested the handcuffs. Definitely no way to slip out of them. She'd just have to drag her gurney with her to find something to help her break out of them. That was her first order of business.

Pulling the gurney behind her, she went to the drawers and pulled open the top one. Gauze. Breathing tubes. Nothing that would help with handcuffs. All she needed was a medical tool, something small enough to fit inside the handcuff tumblers. If she could find one, she'd be free.

But her alone time was cut short when a nurse walked in.

"You shouldn't be up," she said, her no-nonsense voice rising. "Let's get back to bed." She approached Brenna carefully as if she was a wild animal. "Just stay calm."

Brenna shook her head, wanting to reassure the woman. "I've been falsely accused. I've never hurt anyone in my life." The tears that threatened earlier would work to her advantage now. If she could win the nurse's sympathy, she might be willing to help.

"I believe you." But from the nurse's tone she was obviously just placating Brenna. "Everyone is your friend here. We just want to help you."

"This isn't what you think," Brenna began. Should she tip her hand? Tell the nurse what was really going on? Apparently Nazer had already said something to the staff about her mental state. If she spoke up, would that sign John's death warrant? It wasn't worth the risk.

"The doctor explained everything," the nurse said, moving a bit closer. "He'll be very upset to find out you weren't in bed, and he'll be phoning in to check on you momentarily so let's get you taken care of and not make him come back to your room, okay?"

Brenna nearly shuddered. She definitely didn't want Nazer coming back. "Can I use the bathroom first?" Not the most original improvisation, but it would do.

The nurse bit her lip, her need to take care of a patient obviously warring with Nazer's orders. "That should be fine. It's right through here." The nurse pointed to a door in the corner of the room. "I'll help you."

Brenna pointed to the handcuff. "I need to be let out." The nurse looked undecided, so Brenna pressed harder. "I won't be long, I promise."

The nurse shook her head. Brenna had pushed too far. "Let me call the guard."

Brenna wanted to call her back, but that would look suspicious. She couldn't do anything while handcuffed to a bed. If she had to have the guard in the room to get the cuffs off, she'd still be free. It would be harder to escape, yes, but she would have accomplished her goal.

The guard appeared from behind the curtain, as big and ferocious-looking as Saabir. Brenna cowered beside the gurney. Better for him to think her weak. Frankly, it wasn't much of an act. She *was* weak, though her muddled mind was starting to clear.

"She needs to use the facilities." The nurse nodded to the bathroom behind her. "I'll be with her the entire time, so could you please uncuff her for a moment?"

He looked her over, and Brenna tried to look as small and terrified as she could. With one last pointed stare, he uncuffed her. Brenna rubbed her wrist, the room starting to spin again, and she swayed.

The nurse caught her around the waist. "Easy there."

And that's when Brenna felt it. A cell phone in the nurse's front pocket. "Thank you," Brenna murmured.

They walked slowly toward the bathroom, Brenna leaning heavily on the woman, knowing the guard was still watching. Before they made it to the door, Brenna stumbled again, carefully pickpocketing and palming the nurse's phone. "I'm so sorry."

The nurse righted herself, careful to keep a hand on Brenna's waist. "It's fine. Are you sure you'll be okay on your own?"

"I'll be fine." Brenna took hold of the metal bar next to the sink. "Don't worry."

The nurse carefully moved around her inside the bathroom, checking to make sure everything was as it should be. "You can close the door, but pull the emergency cord if you need anything else. I'll be right out here." She walked back out and leaned against the wall to give Brenna a semblance of privacy.

Brenna gave her a feeble nod as the door closed. Quickly dialing the emergency number for Griffin Force that would start a trace on her location, she held it to her ear, waiting for it to connect. When she heard the familiar beep, she entered in her specific agent code with 911 at the end. With any luck, Julian and Colt would find her and send reinforcements. Nazer's little plan would be over before it started.

She used the facilities, knowing there might not be another chance for a long while. When she emerged, she kept up her act of being weak and dizzy and sagged against the wall. The nurse immediately came over and put her arm around her again. Brenna slipped the phone back inside the woman's pocket. Hopefully she wouldn't be any the wiser.

"Thank you," Brenna murmured again as she was led back to the gurney.

Once she was situated, the guard cuffed her again. Before he left to take up his post outside the door, a small two-way radio crackled at his belt. He unclipped it and spoke in Pashto. *"Hao."*

He listened for a moment, but Brenna couldn't hear exactly what Nazer was saying. "I'll bring her right down," he continued, his Pashto flawless. He was obviously a native of that region of Afghanistan.

Her stomach sank at the transfer taking place already. There was a good chance Julian hadn't even received her coded emergency call yet. The nurse covered her with a blanket and the guard started to push the gurney into the hall. "The ambulance is ready to transport her now," he said, his English low and gruff, but understandable.

The nurse patted her arm. "Good luck," she said, her eyes softened with compassion.

Brenna nodded. "Thanks again."

If she said anything to the nurse it could put her and John in danger when Nazer found out. She had to trust that her message to Julian was received.

The guard wheeled her through several hallways until they came to something that looked more like a loading dock than a patient area. An ambulance was parked there and a large truck was getting medical waste loaded onto it. Brenna watched for a moment, trying to figure out Nazer's endgame. It wasn't until she saw the containers with protective casings being carried toward the truck that it all became very clear.

That was radioactive waste.

Since it was a hospital, with cancer-treating equipment, they would probably have been using cobalt, one of the deadliest materials that could be used to make a dirty bomb. A crude one, but definitely a bomb that would cause a lot of damage for years to come.

She clenched her teeth, pulling on her handcuff. "Find me, Julian," she whispered to herself, hating that she had to lie there helpless and watch. The scene played out in front of her in slow motion. The surprised look on the faces of the two men shot where they stood. The driver's attempt to run from the cab only to be mercilessly chased down and killed. It was like a horrible loop on repeat through her mind.

Nazer and two other men dragged their bodies behind the pile of waste containers the men hadn't loaded yet. "Let's move," Nazer said. The two men next to him got into the truck carrying the cobalt. Her guard uncuffed her and she slid off the gurney. He took her arm and started to lead her to the ambulance.

She had to do something.

Stomping on his instep, she whirled around and ran for the fire alarm. After pulling it, she was relieved to hear the high-pitched squeal. Maybe the diversion would give her enough of a distraction. Heading for the truck, she was about to slip out the open loading dock door when a shot rang out. The bullet brushed her shoulder, its path burning a trail of heat across her as it touched her skin. She held up her hands, turning around slowly. That had been a warning shot. The next one wouldn't miss. If she wanted to stay alive, she didn't have another choice, but to stay where she stood.

"I told you what would happen if you didn't do exactly what I said." Nazer had to yell over the fire alarm, but she heard him loud and clear. Even if she hadn't, he held her brother's picture in one hand, a phone in the other. "This is your one and only warning. The next time, you'll both be dead."

The guard stalked toward her, grabbing her newly injured arm and yanking her along with him. She was shoved in the front of the ambulance, and Nazer climbed in next to her to drive.

The scenery around her wasn't distinctive enough to give anyone directions, but Brenna watched it closely, just in case. It gave her mind something else to think about besides being stuck between the men who'd just murdered three people. She swallowed the bile in her throat. Their depravity seeped into the cab of the ambulance as surely as the cobalt in the back was giving off dangerous radioactivity. She pressed her back into the seat to put as much distance as she could between them. How much longer?

After half an hour, they drove into an area with houses set back from the road, with a few in fields. The ambulance finally pulled up in front of an older farmhouse, the stolen truck filled with radioactive cases right behind them.

Nazer jumped down and pulled her across the seat. She nearly fell out of the ambulance, her body's muscles protesting at the harsh treatment. He gave her a disgusted look. "At least your destiny in my organization will give your life meaning."

"You being captured will give my life meaning." She raised her chin. "You haven't won yet."

He grasped her chin so hard, tears sprang to her eyes. "But I will. And there's nothing you can do about it."

Brenna pushed away from him, stumbling backward, but she held her ground. She wasn't going to give up. Not now. Not until the moment she took her last breath. And hopefully that wouldn't be anytime soon.

CHAPTER FIFTEEN

C olt strode into a hospital full of chaos. Police swarmed the hallways, along with Counter-Terrorism Command and British Secret Intelligence Service. The place was filled with people, but Colt only wanted to see one person. Brenna.

When her emergency code had activated, it was the sweetest feeling of relief Colt had ever felt. She was alive and in a position to send an SOS. All they had to do now was find that phone. The trace on it was steady and he knew she was in this hospital somewhere.

Julian was just ahead of him, his steps matching Colt's. They both were anxious to get to her, to make sure she was safe. Several law enforcement agents gave them a look as they passed, but a man who was obviously in charge stopped them. "Mr. Bennet, what are you doing here?"

Julian stuck out his hand and the other man shook it. "Mr.

Sinclair, one of my people is in this building and it's urgent that we find her."

Mr. Sinclair shook his head. "Sorry, but we can't have you traipsing all over this hospital. We have a national security situation here and no non-essential personnel are permitted." His eyebrows drew downward. "In fact, how did you get this far?"

Julian ignored that question. "The woman I'm trying to find is in company with Nazer al-Raimi." His voice was quiet, but his words carried weight.

Mr. Sinclair stared for just a moment, then let out a breath. "You better tell me what this is all about." He motioned toward an empty patient room behind him. "Let's take it in there."

Colt bit the inside of his cheek. He didn't want to talk, he just wanted to find her. The longer they waited, the more time Nazer had to spirit her away. Julian must have felt his frustration because he turned to give Colt a little nod as if to say, *I know*, which was a bit of a relief.

Once they were in the tiny exam room, Mr. Sinclair turned around. "What's going on?"

Julian put his hands in his pockets. He always seemed to do that when he was giving out important details. "An associate of mine was kidnapped by Nazer and she sent out an SOS code. We traced it here and we need to find her, fast."

Mr. Sinclair gave Julian a once-over as he weighed his answer. Surprisingly, even though they'd been in the air for hours on their way from Afghanistan, Julian still looked put together, his suit barely rumpled. Colt had managed to get some sleep on the plane, but he felt like a crumpled piece of paper who'd been tossed in a garbage can, fished out, and tossed in again.

"Nazer al-Raimi makes every situation a little more danger-ous." Mr. Sinclair ran a hand over his face. "An hour ago, a truck carrying discontinued equipment that had been used to treat cancer was hijacked."

"Why would that bring out every law enforcement agency in the city?" Colt asked.

"Because part of that load was Cobalt-60."

It was hard for Colt not to let his jaw fall to the floor. That's what this whole thing had been about. "He's going to make a dirty bomb."

"We're running through security footage now and talking to anyone who might have seen anything, but it's been slow going. With Nazer being involved we have a solid direction to go in." Mr. Sinclair straightened. "Do you have any other information that may be helpful?"

"The woman he's with is transmitting a signal from this hospital. If we find her, we find him." Colt turned toward the door. "I say we get to it."

Mr. Sinclair and Julian exchanged a look, but didn't contra-dict him. They followed him back into the hallway. "Where to now?" Sinclair asked.

Julian took out his phone. "Augie just sent me the new coor-dinates of the trace. She's on the second floor, south wing." He started in that direction, quickening his steps. Colt was glad they were finally doing something.

As they walked past a group of officers, Sinclair tapped one on the shoulder. "Come with me," he ordered and the man did so without a word. The four of them headed up to the second floor, following Julian's lead. He glanced down at his phone for updates, but mostly he was doing the same thing Colt was—scouring the area for Brenna.

When they'd narrowed it down to one patient room, the men drew their weapons. Julian gave the go signal and they burst in, but there was only a nurse inside, tapping away at a computer terminal.

"Step back," Sinclair yelled. "Slowly raise your hands."

The nurse looked up with wide eyes and did what she was told. "What's going on?"

"We're looking for a woman. Brown hair, hazel eyes. She was here about an hour ago." Colt searched the room, pushing back the curtain, looking in the bathroom. Brenna wasn't here. Was it another one of Nazer's tricks?

The woman looked between the men. "I see a lot of patients every day. That describes about half of them."

She looked sincere, but Colt couldn't trust anyone right now. "Show me your phone."

The nurse tilted her head, surprised by the request, but she complied. She took it out of her pocket and gave it to him. Colt pulled up the call history and Brenna's codes were there. He turned the screen around and showed it to her. "A call was made from this phone an hour ago. We traced that to the woman we're searching for. Can you tell us anything?"

The nurse stared at the screen. "I was helping a woman who was being held for transport to Broadmoor Psychiatric hospital. She must have taken my phone and dialed that number."

"Tell me everything you remember about her." Colt had to know what her condition was, find a clue to what was going on.

"She was dizzy from the drugs she'd been given. They kept her sedated before she got here."

Probably the same stuff they'd given him. Colt and Julian were lucky she'd been coherent enough to get the phone and type in the code at all.

The nurse continued, her voice careful and calm. She was obviously used to high pressure situations. "The guard came in and uncuffed her so she could use the facilities."

"She was handcuffed? Why would they do that?" Sinclair put in.

"I assume because she was a criminal." The nurse shrugged. "I didn't ask a lot of questions. The doctor treating her asked for the guard to bring her to the ambulance bay where she was going to be transported, so he cuffed her back up and went on his way. That's the last I saw of her." The nurse hesitated. "Just before he wheeled her away, though, she thanked me. I thought that was odd to be thanked by someone who had killed so many people."

He clenched his fist, wanting to tell her the kind of woman Brenna was. It didn't surprise him that she'd thanked her before going to her certain death with a terrorist, but he kept quiet. It wouldn't do any good anyway. Frustration hit Colt like a punch to the gut.

She was already gone.

They'd been so close.

Nazer had gotten away with Brenna, a load of Cobalt-60, and he was going to set off a dirty bomb. There was no question he'd kill her along with anyone else who got in the way.

Julian glanced at him, but when Colt didn't say anything else, he stepped forward. "We'll need to keep your phone for the time being. Our tech guy might be able to get some more clues from it."

She didn't look pleased, but didn't make a verbal protest. It wasn't like she had a choice anyway. "I hope you find her."

"We will." The more Colt said it out loud the better he felt. They were going to find her.

Julian turned to Sinclair, his mind going to the next step. "Was there anything in the loading bay?"

Sinclair led them out to the nurse's station and down the hall. "Preliminary reports are that the driver and two workers were all found dead. Someone pulled the fire alarm from down there and that was what gave us a place to start."

That had to have been Brenna. She was leaving them a trail of bread crumbs. The glimmer of hope Colt had been holding onto flickered brighter. "Can you take us down there?" He spoke to Sinclair, but looked in Julian's direction as he did it. He didn't want to step on anyone's toes, but the sooner they figured this out, the sooner they'd get Brenna back.

Neither Sinclair nor Julian seemed to mind. "Sure," Sinclair said.

They followed the maze of hallways until they came to the back of the hospital. Police were everywhere here as well, yet Sinclair cleared the way for them pretty easily. Colt would have to ask Julian who this guy was later.

A coroner was with the dead bodies, so Colt bypassed those. He went straight for the abandoned gurney near the loading bay. Handcuffs still dangled from one side reminding him how close they'd been to finding her.

"Has the surveillance footage shown anything?" he asked, needing to see her alive even if it was on a screen.

"It's just coming in now." A man in a dark suit was

approaching and he handed Sinclair an iPad. "Here's what we've got."

They all crowded around the small screen and saw the two workers shot first, then the driver. Colt could see the gurney in the corner of the screen, but it didn't show Brenna's face, only her lower body. She came into full view, however, when the guard had her by the arm and was hustling her toward the ambulance. If Colt had blinked he would have missed her stomping on the guard's foot to get away long enough to pull the fire alarm. *That's my girl*, he nearly said out loud, but caught himself just in time. She'd almost escaped, but for some reason, she stopped and turned around.

"Can we pause it there?" Colt asked.

"What made her stop?" Sinclair squinted down at the screen, pulling it closer to his face.

"Enlarge it there?" Julian pointed to the top corner.

Sinclair enlarged it as much as he could. Nazer was holding something in his hand, but it was in shadow. He held it out to Brenna and kept talking, but there was no audio. He had something on her, that much was obvious.

"Can you tell what it is?" If he was threatening her with something, Colt had to know what it was.

Sinclair couldn't enlarge it any further. "A paper? A picture? I can't tell. I'll get one of my techs on it."

"Can I send it to Augie as well?" Julian asked, his eyes still on the iPad screen. His gaze was intense, as if he could stare right through the footage and find the clue they needed to bring her home. "He's pretty handy with stuff like this."

Sinclair gave him a long look, but nodded. "You're going to owe me."

"If we catch Nazer before he sets off a dirty bomb, we all win," Julian said quietly.

Colt looked out at the bay doors. "Do we have any idea where he might have gone?"

"None. We put out an APW so every law enforcement agency in Britain is looking for the truck. Now we can add Nazer's picture to it." Sinclair shook his head. "I'm going to need every piece of information you've got on this case, Bennet. And I mean everything."

Julian let out a breath, pulling his attention back to the men surrounding him. "Let's go back to your office. I'm sure with the possibility of a dirty bomb being released in London, you'll have a lot of agencies to notify and direct."

"Where's his office?" Colt didn't want to leave the hospital just yet. He wanted to question more of the staff, look around the loading dock some more. There could be an overlooked clue that would point them to where Nazer had taken Brenna.

"I guess I didn't introduce the two of you, did I?" Julian turned to Sinclair. "Colt Mitchell, this is William Sinclair, chief of the British SIS. William, this is Colt Mitchell, former member of the Canadian Joint Task Force 2 and currently a member of Griffin Force."

Colt put out a hand, completely taken aback. "I'm surprised to see you in the field, sir." Did chiefs of anything ever come out of their offices? In Colt's experience, they were mostly pencil pushers.

"I'm a hands-on sort of guy," Sinclair said. "And when Cobalt-60 goes missing, I should definitely be in the field." He turned to Julian. "Let's go. We can talk on the ride over."

Colt spoke up. "I'd like to stay here, do a little investigating on my own."

Julian looked at Sinclair. "Would that be okay? He's one of my best."

"It's fine. Just don't get in the way."

Colt watched them pick their way over to the loading dock, their heads already put together and deep in conversation. His hand found its way to the side of the gurney. She was alive. Leaving them clues.

He closed his eyes for a moment, visualizing the footage Sinclair had shown them. Brenna had pulled the alarm. Stopped to face Nazer. He could see the moment when she knew she was beat and let the guard take her arm again. They'd hustled her to the ambulance and forced her inside. Was anyone looking for the ambulance? Those would stick out a bit, right? And then it hit him. Most ambulances were fitted with GPS. And that could be traced.

He took out his cell phone. "Augie, I need you to find something for me."

He walked back through the hallways the way they'd come, his step in between a fast walk and a run as he headed for their car. He wasn't beaten yet.

CHAPTER SIXTEEN

Brenna was in a small, cramped kitchen. In any other situation she might have found the home cozy and warm, but with a burly guard sitting next to her at a table so tiny their knees touched, it seemed more irritating—bordering on disturbing, than anything else. There wouldn't be a chance for escape here.

She watched the two other men going in and out to carefully load three suitcases into a car parked behind the house. If they were filled with TATP like Brenna suspected, they had good reason to be careful. TATP was so unstable, it could blow up and kill them all.

The moment they'd walked in the house, Nazer had gone immediately to the back with a nerdy looking man wearing glasses and a bow tie. The two containers with the protective casings had been brought in and disappeared into the same room as Nazer and his nerd friend. She hadn't seen either of them for awhile, but she had an idea of what was going on. It was silly to hope that there wasn't a dirty bomb already put together with only the radioactive part missing. Nazer was nothing if not prepared. But the good news was, with Cobalt-60 they still had to convert the compound's shards into inhalable particles. That could take a while, right? Maybe enough time for someone to figure out what was going on, or best case scenario, for Colt and Julian to find her.

With another glance around the house looking for a clock, she turned to her table companion. "Do you know what time it is?" It had to be late afternoon. Her guard didn't answer. "Can you tell me how long we're going to be here?" Did he even know what Nazer was doing in that back room?

He stared at her, his eyes shrewd. "Are you in such a hurry to die?"

"Why does anyone have to die?" She shifted in her chair, her arm beginning to throb from the bullet graze. He jumped a bit at her movement, his hand going to his shoulder holster. She held up her palms. "Relax. This chair is just uncomfortable. I'm not trying to go anywhere." Leaning an elbow on the table, she turned toward him. "Why not just walk away before anyone gets hurt?"

"We must fight against the coalitions who fight against us. We are at war." He leaned forward until he was so close to her face she could smell a strong odor of coffee and tobacco on his breath. "The Islamic State is being bombed daily by Britain, U.S., France, Spain and others. Our men are dying. Why wouldn't we fight back against those who attack us?"

Brenna inched her head back a bit to avoid smelling his bad breath. "Nazer only cares about himself. He doesn't care about who is bombing the Islamic state."

The guard slapped his hand on the table, startling her. "We will purify the world. And Nazer is the one who can unite us."

She frowned. That was a dangerous line of thinking, and there was no doubt Nazer would encourage that. "You think Nazer can unite ISIS with AQIM? He's insignificant to the leadership. Small man on the bottom rung of the ladder."

He glared at her. "Our leaders listen to him. They know we will be stronger if we can unite. Nazer brings everyone to the table who wants the world to recognize that we have a legitimate state to call our own."

Brenna snorted. "A legitimate state? One you took by violence and war. Your leaders have killed anyone who opposed them."

"Every country has a story. A struggle. But we will be bringing the world pure religion. Something you couldn't understand."

He was getting agitated and Brenna knew she should stop, but couldn't help herself. "You're right, I don't understand it."

The guard was about to say more, his index finger pointed toward her chest, but Nazer came into the room and clapped a hand on his shoulder. "We are ready, Ayman. The time is at hand."

Ayman stood, stumbling a bit as he tried to extricate his legs from underneath the small table. "I stand with you."

Nazer looked gratified, bending his head a little in acknowledgment. "Call the others."

The two other men and bow-tie guy quickly assembled in the kitchen. Nazer stood in front, and from Brenna's vantage point, the bright sunshine coming through the window behind gave him a near halo. But she knew firsthand he was no angel.

"Each of you has been sent your target coordinates." He held up his phone. "When you reach your objective, wait for my signal. Then will come your moment of glory!"

"Glory!" They all cheered and their shouts shook Brenna to the core. They were celebrating and raising their hands over their own death and the destruction they would leave behind. It was sickening.

They began to disperse, heading to the cars outside and Nazer walked over to the table where she sat, his grin triumphant. "We've been preparing for this day for a long time."

"So have we." She raised her chin with false bravado. "You won't get near the Parliament buildings."

"With what I've got in mind, we don't need to be all that near." All his good humor drained from his face and the cold mask he'd always shown her was back. "You'll be taking a drive with me."

Brenna had anticipated being forced to go along on one of the attacks, but hearing the words spoken aloud made it real. Bile rose in her throat, but she choked it back. There had to be a chance between now and the bomb detonation where she could make a difference. If she couldn't stop it altogether, maybe she could lessen the damage somehow. She had to try. "Where are we going?"

Nazer waved a hand. "Be patient. You'll get your final instructions once you're in the van."

One of the men who'd been loading the suitcases entered the room, his breathing labored. Had he handled the Cobalt-60? Were they even using protective gear? *Suicide bombers probably don't think about stuff like that before a mission.*

They were quickly coming to the end and it didn't look like anyone was going to find her.

"There is a car approaching." The smaller man's words made Brenna's head snap up. Had she heard him correctly? There shouldn't be anyone approaching. Her heart lifted. Someone had figured things out!

Nazer frowned and moved to the window. He parted the curtains and watched the black sedan make its way down the drive. "Detain them. We can't let anything ruin our timetable."

The man nodded and stepped back out. "It's probably a curious local." Nazer sounded like he was trying to reassure himself, but Brenna could see the concern in his eyes. Nazer had chosen this farmhouse because of its isolation.

Nazer began to pace, becoming more agitated with each turn around the kitchen. Brenna's heart thumped wildly, hoping she was right and that Griffin Force was on its way. They both snapped to attention when they heard gunfire. *Pop, pop, pop.*

Brenna rose from her chair, but Nazer drew his gun. "Sit back down."

She did, but not before she glimpsed someone running toward the house. Nazer must have seen them, too. He walked out the back door, his gun drawn. "Stay there. If I see you outside, I'll shoot you." he ordered as he went down the back porch steps.

She didn't even wait for him to clear the porch before she headed for the front door. If Griffin Force was here, she wanted to be out there with them. Throwing open the front door, she nearly collided with the man being shoved through it. "Colt!"

She backed up, trying to regain her footing. Watching the

men in front of her was like seeing her nightmares come to life. Ayman had a gun to the back of Colt's head and he looked ready to pull the trigger. Nazer was striding up behind them, a conquering swagger in his steps. "What an interesting development," Nazer said as he looked between her and Colt. "Where's the rest of Griffin Force?"

"I'm alone." Colt's gaze pierced her to the core as if willing her to understand.

No. This couldn't be happening. He wouldn't come alone. Where was Julian? Where was the rest of the team? She looked past Colt to the empty driveway, then met his eyes. She couldn't hold back the question. "Why?"

"I had to find you." Colt's eyes raked over her and she could feel him taking an assessment of her injuries. She gave him a nod to let him know everything was okay, except for the fact he'd come alone. Now they were both at Nazer's mercy. Again.

"Nazer, it's not too late. Just let her go." Colt's voice was commanding and clear, his years of experience as a leader shining through.

"It feels like we've been here before." Nazer knit his brows together. "But we're not in a burning building this time and she's not just a prisoner, is she? She's important to you. That's why you've come alone."

Brenna held her breath. Somehow she'd held out hope that Nazer wouldn't have guessed how vulnerable they really were. He wouldn't hesitate to use that against them. Dread rocketed through her insides.

"Yes. I care a great deal for her." Colt tilted his head and lifted his shoulders, his eyes never leaving hers. "I don't know how she feels, and wish I could tell her under different circumstances, but I never stopped caring, even after she left me."

Was this a cover story? What was really going on? The circumstances couldn't be less romantic. They were in a terrorists' lair, possibly facing their own death, and yet all of that faded away and it was only Colt's face she saw. If it was a cover story, she wanted to believe it. Her heart flipped over in her chest. It made sense he would use their history to make a story more believable, but there was no way she could play along when her true feelings were so easy to see.

"Colt," she said softly. "I've wanted to tell you for so long how sorry I was. I shouldn't have left you."

She wanted to go to him so badly and even took a step forward, but Nazer grabbed her arm. His hand startled her, and Brenna barely had time to blink before he backhanded her across the face. She fell to the floor and he stood over her, screaming. "I knew it! You're just like all the others—a temptress, a tease. You leave the men when you owe loyalty!"

With a roar, Colt broke free of Ayman and tore across the room, slamming Nazer to the ground next to Brenna. She scrambled out of the way as Colt began punching Nazer with a fury she'd never seen before. His face was twisted in rage and Nazer tried to fight back. Colt definitely had the upper hand until Ayman joined the fray.

With the gun planted in his face, Colt had no choice but to back up, his hands raised. "Touch her again and I'll kill you," he breathed.

Brenna's cheek felt like it was on fire, but she stood next to Colt and reached out to take his hand. Standing there to face Nazer together gave her a strength she didn't realize she had.

Nazer only sneered at them. "Of course a weak man would take her back, but I'm afraid we don't have any time for hugs and kisses," he hissed. "The timetable just moved up since Griffin Force can't be far behind. Not for long, though. Soon your task force will only be a memory."

Colt's face was flushed and he was breathing hard, but he stood firm and his voice was calm. "Last time we were in a standoff like this, you offered a deal."

Nazer touched the bridge of his nose as if recalling exactly how he'd gotten those bruises. He didn't look in the mood to negotiate anything. "No deal. You'll do what I say or I'll kill her while you watch."

Colt's jaw clenched. "You're making a mistake."

"I don't think so." He flicked a glance to Ayman and he jumped forward to pat Colt down. Colt stood motionless, staring a hole in Nazer's head, but the only thing taken from him was a phone. Ayman removed the battery and smashed the rest of it on the floor.

Once it was done, Nazer motioned to Brenna with his gun. "It's time to go. You'll have to leave him once again like the faithless woman you are."

"You don't know the first thing about me." Brenna's hand tightened on Colt's. She wanted to hug him, but without taking her eyes off of an unpredictable terrorist, the most she could do was press her side against his. It was a dangerous game, but even if Colt were playing some sort of cover story about caring for her, she would hold those words close for a long time to come.

Colt kept her next to him, pulling her forward, with his hand out in a conciliatory gesture. "Okay, I have a deal you can't refuse this time, Nazer. You get two for one. I'll go with her. Whatever you have planned, let us do it together."

Brenna heart rate tripped over itself. He sounded so sincere. If this was part of his cover, she couldn't tell.

Nazer tapped his gun on his thigh, one hand holding his ribs like he was in pain, too. *Good.* "Now that's an unexpected offer." He stepped back, giving Colt a once-over, his eyes shrewd. "I think you might be a little too conspicuous for what we have planned, though."

"I can blend in. That's my job, after all." Colt took another step toward him. "The Parliament buildings always have a lot of people milling around. No one's going to notice one more guy."

Nazer contemplated that, stroking his beard, his other hand never leaving his ribs. Had one been broken? Brenna hoped so. "I wouldn't mind having two Griffin Force members setting off the bomb. Hmm…" He looked at his watch. "Ayman, go make sure everything is secure. Make sure your vest is on and ready. We have to stay ahead of the timetable now."

Ayman bowed his newly bald head. He was definitely a disciple of Nazer's who had been told that being ready for battle meant you shaved all your hair. "Yes, sir." He took keys out of his pocket as he headed for the driveway.

With just the three of them, the thought crossed Brenna's mind that maybe they could try to overpower Nazer. But he must have had the same idea because he trained his gun on them once more. "Don't do anything hasty. You know what will happen if you do."

"I think you've made it pretty clear our lives are on the line." Colt frowned when Brenna shook her head. "What? What else is going to happen?" He moved slightly in front of her as if to shield her from the answer. When she could only look at him, her words obviously failing her, his fingers gave hers a reassuring squeeze.

Her chin lowered to her chest. "He's got someone watching my brother. If I don't do what he says, he'll give the kill order." Brenna could barely get the words out. Emotion welled in her remembering the one time she'd taken Colt home to meet her family. John would have been around fifteen then, anxious to enlist and hero-worshipping anyone who had been in the military. He'd followed Colt around the entire visit and they'd really hit it off. At least now Colt would understand why she couldn't leave, couldn't risk her little brother.

"Well, that makes things a little more clear." Colt didn't seem ruffled, instead his grip felt stronger. "Don't worry, we're going to figure this out."

Nazer pointed the weapon at his chest, disgust lacing his voice. "Yes, she should definitely worry. And so should you. I have no problem killing you here and taking her to the target alone."

Colt raised his free hand to placate Nazer. "I'm unarmed."

"Which makes you an easy target." Nazer backed up and opened the door. "Time to get in the van. Both of you."

Nazer was only a few steps ahead of them, but he didn't need to watch them every second with the leverage he had. Colt slipped his arm around her shoulders and pulled her against his side. "It's going to be okay, I promise."

She let herself be held. Was this going to be the last time? "Thanks for coming for me."

They stopped in front of the van. Ayman stood next to the

driver's side door and gave Nazer a smart salute. A loyal follower to the end.

Nazer returned the gesture. "You'll ride in the back and make sure everything stays where it should until we unload it."

That didn't sound like they were especially sure of their loading abilities. A prickle of warning slithered up her back.

"Yes, sir." Ayman said as he walked toward the back of the van. Brenna shook her head. The other cars were already gone and could very well be in position right now. Could they stop what was already in motion?

They were about to find out. Nazer opened the back of the van. "Get in."

CHAPTER SEVENTEEN

Colt could feel the tremble that went through Brenna as she turned in his arms. "Shh, just stay close."

"He's not going to allow us to stay together." Her eyes were on Nazer who was inspecting the bomb in the back.

Colt flexed his hand. He didn't regret letting Nazer know in no uncertain terms that he wouldn't allow Brenna to be hurt, but he had to stay focused if he was going to get them out of this.

He pulled her to him, wanting to tell her what was really going on, but knowing with Nazer near he couldn't. He bent to her ear to at least give her a heads up. "Just be patient. I have a plan."

He knew she'd heard him when her arms tightened around him. She lifted her face and he could see the question in her eyes that she couldn't ask. "Okay," was all she said.

"Hurry up. You can say your goodbyes later," Nazer snarled. Colt led her to the van, feeling like they were marching to the gallows. He didn't dare look around or adjust the earpiece in his ear. Hopefully the cavalry was close.

Nazer threw Colt the keys to the van. "You drive so I can keep an eye on you."

Colt caught them, but winced as they dug into his sore hand. Every bit of pain was worth it, though, when he saw Nazer holding his side and the darkening bruise on his cheek. No one was going to touch Brenna like that. Not ever.

He made sure he stayed a step in front of Brenna as they approached the van. If he thought they could get away with it, he'd tell her to run, but it was too risky. Nazer had all his bases covered with her brother under watch and a gun on them. He couldn't take a chance of her being shot.

"You'll sit right behind me in the passenger seat so I can get to you any time I want." He pointed to Brenna with his gun, making Colt's heart rate trip over itself. It was a solemn reminder that if he didn't play this right, Brenna would die. He had to be careful. With one last look around the yard and surrounding field, he opened the side door of the white van for Brenna.

It was going to be a tight fit. The dirty bomb was in a case and taking up most of the room in the back. Ayman was in the bottom left corner, taking up every inch of available space there. Brenna squeezed in where Nazer had said. At least he'd still be able to see her while he was driving.

She glanced at Colt as she sat down. "This is going to be cozy." She wrinkled her nose. There was an acidic smell coming from the case. Being this close couldn't be good, but there weren't a lot of other options. Hopefully the protective casing that surrounded it would be enough to protect them from exposure to any radioactivity.

Colt tried to give her a reassuring smile. "It's going to be okay. Trust me."

"I do." She looked up at him with so much confidence in her eyes, his heart squeezed. Part of her had to think that he was playing a cover, but the moment he could, he would tell her there wasn't anything fake about what he'd said. Then he'd be free to ask her what her feelings were. Was she just going along because that's what was expected? He hoped not. If she still cared, the minute this was over, he was going to take her somewhere safe where he could just hold her. And kiss her.

Nazer reached in and took a small black detonator off the casing. "Wouldn't want to be without this." He held it up, the pen-like trigger giving him enough power to bring a triumphant smile to his face. "I've waited so long."

Colt shook his head at the unbalanced look in Nazer's eyes. There wouldn't be a chance to disrupt Nazer's plans here. They needed to get going. He walked around toward the driver's side and the movement snapped Nazer back to attention. "Let's go, then."

Nazer lifted the detonator and waved it toward Colt. "If you do anything or your Griffin Force friends show up, I'll press it. This town and all the people in it would be dealing with fallout for years to come."

That's what worried him. Colt opened the door. "Don't worry. No one's showing up. I'm here for her, that's it." And it wasn't a line. He was here for her, but only because he wanted to get her out of it, not die along with her.

He got in and started the van, cracking a window to relieve the overwhelming smell. With a quick glance at Brenna, he wasn't surprised to see her trying to surreptitiously get a good look at the device's explosives outside of the protective casing. He put the van into drive and headed toward the street. *Good girl*, he thought. Maybe she could get a read on it and figure out how to disarm it.

Nazer had set his gun in his lap and pulled his phone out of his pocket. Colt thought about making a move, but that detonator was still in his other hand.

"Turn left here," he said, glancing up momentarily at the road in front of them.

That was unexpected. Colt furrowed his brow. "But London is that way." He pointed to the right.

"I know." Nazer began tapping icons with a concentrated look on his face. If Colt craned his neck, he could just see a map with pinpoints on it. He was too far away to see the actual locations, though. He tried to catch Brenna's eye to see if she could get a clearer picture. Brenna caught his slight signal and leaned forward as far as she could, but Nazer put the phone to his ear before she could see anything.

"Are you in position?" he asked, his tone authoritative. "We have to do this earlier than we anticipated." He looked at his watch. "Everything should be ready in fifteen minutes. Call me when you're there."

Colt kept his eyes on the road. Was his earpiece working? Had Jake and Julian heard that? He hadn't seen any cars following them and his gut was starting to get the feeling he was in this alone. There should have been a signal of some sort by now. He blew out a breath. He had to stay positive. The team hadn't let him down yet.

He lifted his foot off the gas, but Nazer was quick to point the gun at his side. "Maintain a steady speed. You'll be turning right in about a kilometer."

They were moving down a tree-lined two way street when he finally saw the street sign. "Prestwick Road?" Colt asked, as Nazer scrolled through his phone.

"Just drive," Nazer barked.

Colt threw Nazer an irritated look that was lost on him since he was focused on his phone. Why would they be headed into the country? Was there a big populace in Northwood? *Make yourself useful and pull that map back up,* Colt thought.

As if Nazer had heard his silent command, he pulled up the map again. Colt caught Brenna's eye and she nodded, already leaning forward. He kept his eyes on the road until after he'd made the turn, then glanced back at her. Her eyes were on Ayman for a moment, but then she stretched out her hands out in the shape of a tube. One of the targets was a tube station.

Predictable, Colt thought, *and deadly.* The casualty list would be extensive. But was he planning to hit the Parliament buildings?

Trying to make sure he didn't call attention to his nonverbal conversation with Brenna, he kept his eyes on the small two-lane road for a minute before he looked at her again. As soon as she had his attention, she put her hands on her head as if they were a crown. Colt frowned. Would Nazer dare attack Buckingham Palace? But then, with all the tourists that visited there every day, that would make sense. Had the idea of him going to Parliament just been a decoy then?

Brenna took one last glance at the map and mouthed parliament before leaned back against her seat. From his rearview mirror he could see Ayman was watching her now. She wouldn't get another chance to look over Nazer's shoulder without Ayman seeing it. But maybe knowing that his targets were the tube, Buckingham Palace and the Parliament would be enough. If only they knew where they were headed with the dirty bomb.

"What are you looking at? Just watch the road." Nazer was obsessively checking his watch. "It's almost time," he murmured to himself. Colt was watching his fingers twitch on that detonator. Hopefully he was focused enough not to press that button just yet.

"You know, you don't have to move things up on my account." Colt needed to stall for time. *Get him talking.* "What made you pick England?"

"Shut up."

Well, that conversation had been shorter than he'd wanted. Nazer wasn't in the talking-about-the-plan mood, but Colt didn't give up so easily. "If you're not using this bomb for the Parliament building, what good is it out in the English countryside?"

Nazer raised his gun and twisted around in his seat so it was trained at Brenna's head. "Would you like me to show you what I want to do right now?"

"No, I wouldn't." There wasn't much to say after that. The things he'd witnessed today were going to keep him up at nights for a while.

Prestwick Road seemed to go on forever. The trees were tall and didn't afford a lot of views, so Colt was driving blind as to their destination. Every now and then there was a stone pillar and a fence, or a tract of older style housing. It seemed idyllic, yet these people had no idea a bomb was in their midst, set to destroy their way of life. Colt had seen so much destruction in his time in Special Ops. That was partly why he'd joined Griffin Force. They had the means to act on intel without a lot of bureaucracy and, to Colt, the sooner they ended this war on terror, the better.

Colt kept an eye on the clock above the mute radio. The fifteen minutes was nearly up. As if on cue, Nazer's phone rang. It was early. That couldn't be good. Nazer held it to his ear.

"*Hao*," he said curtly.

Everyone's attention in the van was on Nazer's side of the conversation. He wasn't saying much, but Colt's nerves tightened to the breaking point when he slammed his fist into the dashboard. "He should have been more careful!" he shouted. "What are the casualties?"

Colt looked at Brenna who looked as stricken as he felt. Had one of the bombs gone off? Were they too late?

"Tell everyone the time is here. There will be glory for us all." He ended the call and stared out the window, the detonator tapping on his thigh. "This is your fault," he said finally.

"What's my fault?" Colt spoke quietly. It wouldn't do any good to antagonize him further. Something was wrong. Very, very wrong.

"We moved up the timetable, but Rafeeq didn't make it to the target before his bomb vest went off." Nazer hit the dashboard again. "We should have had more casualties. But at least the police are busy." He looked at Colt. "Soon they will be very busy."

Colt felt his words like a punch to the gut. Casualties. A bomb had gone off. Why did it always feel he was one step behind those who wanted to rain terror down on the innocent? "Which target was hit? The tube station? Parliament buildings? Or was Rafeeq headed for Buckingham palace?" Colt gripped the steering wheel tightly, trying to keep control. How many people's lives would never be the same after today? If only they'd figured it out sooner. Was Griffin Force even hearing this? The urge to check his earpiece was nearly overwhelming, but he couldn't risk Nazer seeing or suspecting he was wired. He had to trust his men and his equipment. But time was running out.

Nazer's mouth was opening and shutting at Colt's accuracy of the attack locations. "How did you know?" He turned to Brenna, the gun back in his hand. "Did you know something?"

She held up her hands, her eyes wide. "No, it wasn't me."

"You forget we captured Saabir." Colt wanted to deflect Nazer's attention away from Brenna. His trigger finger was a little too twitchy.

Nazer slowly turned the gun toward Colt, his mouth hanging open like the air had been sucked from his lungs. "You're lying. He . . .? I just-" He couldn't get out a sentence, but finally swallowed. "I never would have expected Saabir would talk, but there's no other explanation."

Colt kept his eyes on the road. At least the gun was on him and away from her. "The information didn't come easily." He gave a nonchalant shrug with his good shoulder. If only they had a hint of where they were going now. "You never know what you'll say under duress."

Nazer's hand twitched on the detonator. "I was right not to tell anyone the final destination. Not even Saabir. While everyone is busy in London, we'll be at the real target and Britain will think twice about crossing us again."

Colt's blood froze in his veins at Nazer's little speech. If London wasn't the real target, where was it?

A loud bang recoiled through the van and for a split second Colt thought the bomb had detonated. "Brenna!" he shouted. The van careened to the right and he struggled to keep them on the road. "Hold on!"

Colt scrambled to keep control of the car. It was a tire blowout. What were the chances of that when you were transporting a dirty bomb that could go off at any second?

He swerved onto the narrow shoulder and slammed on his brakes, nearly hitting a tree before they came to a stop. He immediately reached back for Brenna and she grabbed his hand. "I'm okay."

He blew out a breath. That's what mattered. "We better see what's wrong." He reached for his door.

"Before we get out, I just want to remind you that if you try anything, I'll just press this detonator." Nazer held it up again. "I can't imagine they'd even have pieces to pick up of either of you if that happened."

"You're willing to die along with us?" Colt knew men like Nazer existed, but somehow he seemed like too much of a narcissist to be a suicide bomber.

"If that's what is required, then yes." Nazer opened the door and got out without a backwards glance back at Colt.

With one more look at Brenna, his heart expanded a little more. She didn't look afraid, only resolved. She was the bravest woman he'd ever known. "Let's get some fresh air, shall we?"

"You don't have to ask me twice," she said as she quickly opened the door.

They all congregated at the front of the van. The right front tire was completely shredded. Nazer was just to Colt's right and his jaw clenched so hard little veins were popping out on his neck. "We're on a timetable!" He glared at his watch as if it were its fault. "Change it. Fast."

"I'm assuming you mean *I* have to change it?" He rolled up his shirtsleeves. Change a tire fast so a terrorist plot can go forward. Now that was something he'd never dreamed of doing. "Where's the spare?"

"Ayman, see if you can still reach it in the back." Nazer stood to the side, looking up and down the street. "Hurry up."

The spare and jack were pulled out with only a little bit of bomb jostling. Colt took it from Ayman, wondering if it was possible to take them both out with it before Nazer pressed down on the detonator. Probably not. *Patience.* He rolled the spare to the front. "This isn't going to be easy, you know."

Nazer's thumb hovered over the detonator, a black scowl on his face. "You've got five minutes to get it done or we're all dead."

There was no doubt in Colt's mind he was telling the truth. He slanted a look at Brenna, who'd moved a few feet behind him. Suddenly changing a tire was a life and death situation. Colt bent to the task.

CHAPTER EIGHTEEN

Brenna watched Colt and Ayman struggle to jack up the van to get the new tire on. Her anxiety increased every time Ayman's suicide vest brushed against something. If that was really made with TATP there was a good chance they were all going to blow up right here. Had she imagined Colt telling her he had a plan? Was this part of it? Out of the corner of her eye she could see Nazer, one hand on his gun and one on the detonator, like a man with two forks who didn't know which one to use.

"Come here," Nazer told her. She touched her still stinging cheek. She didn't want to be anywhere near the man, but there were no alternatives. Walking toward him, she made sure to meet his eyes, knowing he hated that as much as Saabir had. But she wouldn't follow their rules for women anymore.

Once she was in front of him, he took her by the arm and bent to her ear. "Just one more incentive for Captain Mitchell to hurry."

He turned her around, but made sure her back was pressed to his front. Colt had stopped working to watch them, but she shook her head. *Don't take any risks for me*, she wanted to say, but kept quiet. Colt was probably thinking the same thing about her, but they both knew they'd do whatever it took to stop him and the bomb.

Colt bent to wrestle the tire on and he winced every so often. Brenna knew his back had to be killing him with his prior injuries. It was amazing he was still standing with what his body had been put through. *He came for me*. The thought warmed her to the core, in one way, and made her cold with the risk to his own life. This couldn't be the end for them. Not yet.

They were still trying to get the tire on when a car came down the road. Brenna tensed. *Just keep going*, she thought to herself, sending an unspoken message to the driver. They didn't need anyone else for Nazer to use as leverage. But from the looks of things, this was a small town and she knew he would stop. He proved her right when, as soon as the driver saw them, he pulled over. "Hi there! You need a hand?"

Colt looked back at Nazer first before he answered. "I think we've got it, but thanks."

Brenna held her breath, but the guy turned his car off and got out. Brenna's heart sank the moment she saw his army green fatigues. This wasn't good. If he was military, he could very well spook Nazer.

"Let me help. Then you'll be on your way that much faster." He strode toward them, his long legs eating up the distance quickly. As he came around the van, Brenna and Nazer came into view. He gave them a funny look, probably with how awkwardly she was standing with Nazer behind her, but didn't comment on it.

He turned to focus on Colt. "Where are you from? From your accent, I'd say definitely across the pond somewhere."

"Yeah. We're Canadian," Colt confirmed as he straightened and shook his hand. "Just got in for a short visit."

A very short visit, if this goes south, Brenna thought grimly.

"I'm Will," the man said as he bent down to look at the tire well. "You've nearly made a hash of it. Let me guide it on."

Ayman glanced over at Nazer, as if unsure what to do. He was fiddling with the zipper of his jacket that hid his suicide vest.

No, Brenna thought as she watched him. *Don't be hasty. Keep it together.*

"Get rid of him," Nazer murmured under his breath. She could feel impatience rolling off of him, his attention completely diverted to the newcomer.

Brenna took a tiny step away to get a little distance. The detonator was in his right hand, just inches from her own. With his focus elsewhere, would she have an opportunity to grab it? Her fingers twitched. *Easy.*

But Nazer stepped around her and walked toward the good Samaritan. "We don't want to inconvenience you. We're fine."

Will shook his head again as Colt held the tire and he tried to wiggle it into place. "I don't mind," he said with a grunt. "I have a few minutes before I have to report for duty."

Colt's head whipped up to stare at Will. "There's a military installation out here?"

"PJHQ." That was met with a blank look so he explained. "Permanent Joint Headquarters, in Northwood just another few clicks that way." He pointed beyond the trees. "There's quite a few offices, but mostly we're known for heading the war operations center in the United Kingdom."

Brenna's heart started to pound. That's where the bomb was headed. Her eyes flew to Colt's. This might be their only chance to stop the attack. What was his plan?

A buzzing came from Will's pocket and he pulled out a cell phone. "Sir." After a moment's pause, he looked over at Colt. "Near Piccadilly Station? Yes, I'll be right in."

"Is something wrong?" Brenna asked, even though she knew what he was going to say. The explosion. The casualties.

"There was a bombing. Our threat alert was just raised." Will's eyes darted back to Nazer's, then behind him where Ayman was now standing. "I need to go into HQ immediately."

"Actually, Will, I think we'll need you a little longer." Nazer drew his gun from behind his back and held it in front of him. "I can't afford to have any witnesses. Or heroes."

Will's eyes widened and he stepped back. "You're part of it, aren't you?"

"Which is why you shouldn't have stopped." Nazer closed the distance between him and Brenna, coming close to her again. She stiffened as he shoved the gun in her side. "Get that tire changed. Now."

"I'm not going to do anything that would help." His friendly face had twisted in anger as he kept backing up toward his car.

Ayman stopped his progress, clamping his hands around Will's arms like a vise.

"Then you're not useful to me." Nazer trained his gun on Will, but Colt stepped in between them.

"Let's not do anything stupid. We'll just get this tire done."

Colt pulled Will away from Ayman and down until they were both in front of the wheel well. "It's not worth dying over."

Nazer lowered the gun, but kept it ready at his side. "Yes. Finish the tire so I can finish what I started."

Brenna closed her eyes, grateful that Colt had intervened. That had been too close. With Nazer so agitated, he would have killed Will and left him in the ditch without blinking. There had been too many deaths already.

When she opened her eyes again, she glanced downward. Nazer's hand with the detonator was less than a foot away. For just a moment, she visualized elbowing Nazer in the stomach and taking it. If only he didn't have a gun in the other hand.

With the tire finally on, Brenna leaned forward to try and catch Colt's eye. He was looking at the tire, as if assessing it, but she noticed his hand was on his thigh, as he formed some basic military signals. All go, on his count. When he finally did look over at her, she gave the okay signal and glanced at Will. He understood as well.

"Let's get loaded up." Nazer took two steps toward the van when his phone buzzed. He shoved the gun in the back of his pants and took it out, his attention completely consumed by the text he'd gotten. After he'd finished reading, his fingers stabbed at the screen as he texted back. He was angry. Maybe things weren't going well with the rest of them.

She could only hope.

Her muscles were like a loaded spring as she waited for Colt's signal. That detonator would be her first priority. He held up three fingers. Then two. Then one. Go.

Nazer looked up just as Colt rushed him and threw him to the ground. Will had already propelled Ayman into the side of the van and both men were struggling to gain the upper hand. "Brenna. Grab it!" Colt yelled.

The detonator was only an inch from Nazer's hand and he was scrambling out of Colt's grasp for it. Brenna plucked it off the ground and turned to find cover. The van seemed like a bad idea with the bomb inside it, but the trees only hid the houses and she didn't want to lead any violence to these people. She opted to use the van.

Ayman was still on his feet, landing a nice left hook to Will's stomach. He recovered quickly, though, and came back with a right uppercut to Ayman's face. His head snapped back, a loud thunk against the van. He seemed dazed and shoved Will off before he took off running. "I've got him!" Will yelled back at them.

"Be careful, he's got a suicide vest on." Brenna shouted, but she didn't know if Will heard her. He disappeared into the tree-line and Brenna turned back to Colt. He was wrestling for Nazer's gun, the weapon poised in the air above them as they pitted their strength against the other. Colt's muscles were straining and the gun lowered toward him a bit. "No," she breathed.

Her breaths sounded loud in her ears as she moved toward him and time seemed to stop when the gun went off. Colt!

But she couldn't move. The air around her seemed to suck in and whoosh by, leaving a white hot pain in its wake. Her hand flew to her side as she fell to the ground. Before her brain could register what had just happened, an explosion sounded from the road, strong enough to knock them back. *Oh no! Will!*

Brenna lay there on the side of the road, looking up at the

sky. Pulling her hand back, she saw the sticky redness on her fingers. *I've been shot.*

Some trees were on fire and the smoke was making dark swirls in the sky. A "Give Way" sign had fallen over next to her and the ridiculous thought came to her that the Give Way yield sign had really given way. *I'm going into shock*, she thought. The reality of her gunshot wound finally started to sink in.

Things seemed out of proportion after that. She took the detonator out of her pocket and held it in her hand, but it was slippery with her blood. She clasped it tighter. That was one thing she couldn't let out of her possession. Where was Colt? Was Will okay? Coughing, she tried to see if any of them were in her line of sight, but the pain was too much.

"Brenna!" Colt's voice came to her as if he were at the bottom of a very deep well.

Suddenly he was there beside her. She closed her eyes. "Colt." He was looking over her injuries, his face telling her what she didn't want to know. "It's bad, isn't it?"

With a shrug, he dragged his eyes to hers. "I've seen worse." But she could see the tight lines around his mouth. He was trying to make it better for her. "Just stay with me. I'll get you to a hospital. As soon as you're stitched up, maybe we can compare scars. I bet I have one about the same as yours." He took the detonator from her hand and she was glad to be relieved of the responsibility.

"It's a date." She shivered. "It's been so long since I've been cold. All those months in Afghanistan were unbearably hot." Colt was pale as he looked down at her and for a moment, she wondered if he was wounded, too. "Are you okay? Did we get Nazer?"

"He's unconscious. We got him." Colt pulled her to his chest. He was so warm. She wanted to snuggle in and stay there.

"I'm sorry," she whispered.

Colt didn't hear her. He was shouting at someone, but there wasn't anyone there besides the two of them. "If anyone can hear me, she's down. We need an ambulance right now!"

She wanted to reach out and comfort him, but she was so tired. With her eyes closed, she buried her face in Colt's chest. The words "I love you" rose to her lips, but her tongue was thick.

He reached out and clutched her to him. "I'm here," he said into her hair.

Brenna used her last reserve of strength and opened her eyes. "Kiss me," she whispered. If she was going to die, she wanted to have that be her last act on earth.

He looked into her face, his eyes full of anguish. He didn't say a word, but bent, his mouth brushing hers in a kiss so urgent and possessive that it took her breath away. She kissed him back with everything she had, every ounce of energy she had left.

When he pulled back, he kept her close, his hands brushing through her hair. "I love you," he said, his mouth next to her ear. "Please don't go."

"I love you, too." But the darkness pushed out the light and pulled her down until her words echoed in the silence.

CHAPTER NINETEEN

"Can't this thing go any faster?" Colt's eyes were riveted on Brenna, so pale and still on the ambulance gurney. The beeping machines behind her testified that she was still alive, but her pulse was thready. She needed to be in the hospital.

Elliott didn't even glance back at Colt. "We've g-g-got to get this bleeding under control," he murmured to himself. "Hold this." He pulled Colt's hand forward to Brenna's side. "P-p-press here."

It felt good to be doing something. Colt applied pressure to her side wound while Elliott started an IV. "How much longer?"

"Normally Watford hospital is a f-f-few minutes out, but with the bombing, everything is locked down and there's a lot of chaos going on right now." Elliott bent over her arm, checking the tubing. He opened it wide so she could get the fluids as quickly as possible.

Colt's chest was tight as he watched. Elliott's stuttering was always the worst under stress. Was there something he wasn't telling him? *No, Elliott wouldn't do that.*

He counted the seconds in between her breaths. Her whispered request to kiss her before she lost consciousness was burned into his brain. Was she anticipating death? Was that her last request? He wanted to reach out and take her hand, but he didn't want to let up any pressure if it meant the bleeding would start again.

"Has Nate called in yet? Or Julian?" Colt twisted around to direct his question at Jake riding in the passenger seat of the ambulance. The team had backed him up when he'd needed it most, and he was sorry he'd doubted them for even a second. But the guilt that he hadn't kept Brenna safe was crushing. He should have told her he was wired and the team was behind them. He should have told her to run and not look back.

Jake turned, his expression grim. "I just got an update from Julian. They've got a guy cornered at Parliament Square. We're evacuating as quickly as possible, but it's touch and go."

"Is he inside?" Colt asked. After all they'd done to stop the attack, he didn't want them to win.

"No, he's in the courtyard."

Well, that was something. There was less chance of loss of life in a courtyard. "How close are the buildings?"

"Not far enough away considering what that vest is capable of." Jake's phone buzzed and he put it to his ear. "Hello?"

Colt watched Jake's shoulders slump. "How bad?"

Any hope Colt had of it ending peacefully slipped away. He looked down at Brenna who seemed to be slipping away as well. With his hand on her shoulder, he bent to her ear. "Lean on me, Bren. Take my strength."

The heart monitors affirmed that she was fighting, but he knew it was wearing on her. The ambulance sped up again and Colt took it as a good sign. "Not much longer and we'll be at the hospital. They'll have you patched up in no time." He hoped.

Jake ended the phone call. "We've got a situation."

Even Elliott looked up this time. "What's going on? Did he get into Parliament or something?"

"No." Jake shook his head. "He did detonate the vest, but only succeeded in killing himself and blowing out a lot of windows. There are some casualties from the flying glass, but that's it."

"Lucky," was all Colt could think to say. That had been too close, but Nazer's plan hadn't succeeded. Griffin Force and everyone who had been hunting these guys had won today. "What's the situation?"

"MI6 was cleaning up the mess on Prestwick Road. There wasn't anything left of the bomber and by the time they'd secured the area, they couldn't find Nazer or the guard that had been assigned to him." Jake's voice was hollow as if he couldn't believe what he was saying.

"Are you telling me Nazer is gone?" The impact of the words was like a mental bomb inside Colt's head. "He was the high value target there. Why would anyone leave him with one guard?"

"They thought he was unconscious." Jake hung his head. "Nate's taking it pretty hard. He was supervising the removal of the dirty bomb and assumed MI6 was taking care of the rest."

"What are they doing to get him back?" If Brenna weren't lying on a gurney in front of him he'd have them turn around and take him to Prestwick Road. Nazer couldn't get away this time. It was beyond comprehension.

"They've got a perimeter set up, they're searching every house. The residents themselves are reeling from Ayman's bomb that took out half of their neighbor's house."

Colt hadn't heard the extent of the damage from that bomb yet. His entire focal point had been Brenna and getting her to a hospital. "How's Will?"

"You mean our Good Samaritan? He's fine. A few scrapes and burns. I'm sure he'll be in debriefing for a while yet." Jake looked down at his phone as if it would magically give them good news. "He was a hero today, that's for sure."

Colt couldn't agree more. "I couldn't have even attempted to take down Nazer without his help." He wanted to thank Will personally. When Brenna was better they could go together. "How far back were you guys following us?"

"We were about a mile behind you. With that road being so small, we couldn't risk Nazer spotting us. But your tracker was loud and clear." Jake puffed out a breath. "You were brilliant in getting us the locations so we could get men in place to stop the bombers."

He looked down at the woman on the gurney, pride running through him. "That was Brenna. She took the risk to peek at the map." She always seemed to do what needed to be done even at great risk to herself. She was a good agent and if they were given a second chance, he'd tell her that.

"Even though three of the bombs went off, they weren't in any populated areas and casualties were minimal. I'd say that's a pretty big win." Elliott watched the monitors. "We just need one more miracle today."

Those were the words hanging in the air when they pulled up to the hospital. The gurney was whisked inside, a doctor running alongside it. "I'm told she gets top priority. I'm Dr. Sutherland."

Colt silently thanked whomever had given that order as he ran on the opposite side of Dr. Sutherland. Brenna's compress was getting sticky again and he knew the bleeding hadn't stopped. That wasn't a good sign. "Gunshot wound to the stomach. She's lost a lot of blood."

The gurney stopped in front of some double doors for authorized personnel only. Colt was loath to release her, but the doctor put his hand on Colt's. "We'll take it from here."

Colt reluctantly let go of Brenna, not wanting to break that last connection to her. He motioned to Elliott. "Can you stay with her?"

Dr. Sutherland nodded. "As an observer only. I'm sorry, but we've got to get her into the OR."

Colt stepped back. For some reason, having Elliott there made him feel better. He trusted him. Not that Dr. Sutherland wasn't a good doctor, but Brenna deserved the best and Elliott would make sure she got it. "Take good care of her." They pulled the gurney through the doors and he could only watch, helplessness flowing through him. He sucked in a breath and let it out slowly. "Please."

Jake appeared at his side. "It's going to be okay," he said, but his words were hesitant, as if he didn't really believe them, but wanted them to be true.

Colt swallowed the lump in his throat. It had to be. They needed that chance at a future together. They'd earned it.

A nurse approached them. "Sir, the waiting room is right through here. I'll come get you if there's any news."

Colt turned and mechanically headed the direction she'd pointed out. What could he do now but wait? The situation was out of his hands and he hated that, but he had to trust that she'd come back to him. "Fight for me," he breathed out.

He sat down in the plastic chair with his head in his hands. He was more than tired. Beyond exhausted. But he was going to sit here and be strong for Brenna, just like she'd been strong for him. He thought back to Yousef's storeroom and how he knew they'd make it through if they just stuck together. They weren't physically together right now, but emotionally, he felt closer to her now than ever before. He squeezed his eyes shut and pleaded with her from his chair. "Fight, Bren. You can do it." He visualized her smile, her take-charge attitude, her kiss, and somehow he knew she would.

Jake sat down beside him, just as the phone buzzed again. Part of Colt wanted Jake to turn it off, that he couldn't take any more bad news today, but the other part wanted it to be good news that he could hold on to. "Are you going to get that?"

Jake grimaced and answered it. "Hey, Julian." He glanced over at Colt. "We're at Watford in the waiting room. They just took her back." He listened a bit more. "Did Nate have an update?"

The answer took so long Colt sat up. Maybe it really was good news. Had they recaptured Nazer? Now that was the kind of news he wanted Brenna to wake up to.

"Can you let us know the minute Nate checks in?" Jake nodded at whatever Julian was saying. "Thanks. I'll keep you posted." He ended the call.

"Well, did Nate find Nazer?" Colt knew he was impatient, but Jake would understand.

"They found his guard's dead body. Apparently Nazer used the guy's gun and carjacked someone in town. They tracked the vehicle heading toward London and Nate is right behind him." Jake put his hand on Colt's shoulder. "I know it's not the best news, but it's positive. You know Nate, he'll stick with it until the job's done."

That was true. He'd been amazed at Nate's perseverance in tough situations every time he'd been on a team with him. And here he'd been shot in the leg not long ago and he was back in the field already. "If anyone's going to get it done, Nate will." He looked over at the doors where they'd taken Brenna. She was a person that got the job done, too. And if nothing else, they'd proven they could work together. Neither of them would have to give up the jobs they had for a relationship.

"You know, even with all this going on, your fly-by-the-seat-of-your-pants plan worked." Jake raised a brow. "And here you are, the one who's always telling us to plan for contingencies."

Colt looked up as another gurney rolled in, and a doctor came around the far side of the desk to meet them. "What have we got?" he asked the paramedic.

"Bomb victim. First degree burns to the torso and some glass embedded in the head and neck. Vitals stable, though."

The gurney barely stopped as they moved into another area. Colt looked over at Jake, the report to the doctor echoing in his mind. Maybe if he'd planned better, Brenna would be standing beside them and there wouldn't be any victims at all. "Yeah, it kind of worked."

That flurry of phone calls before he'd headed to the farmhouse was a distant memory now. It had been a good skeleton while they figured out the rest as they went. A part of him would always wonder, though, if he should have done things differently.

"No, not kind of. We prevented Nazer's main event." He pointed toward the door that the bomb victim had gone through. "Yes, there were some casualties, but it could have been so much worse. All because you went in alone." Jake nudged his shoulder. "Gutsy."

"I wasn't alone. You guys had my back. As always." Colt meant that. Griffin Force had become his family over the last months. He trusted them.

"It was a risk. You didn't know how Nazer would react, if the tracker and earpiece would be found. You were going in with a lot of faith." Jake leaned in to meet his eye. "It paid off. We took care of business."

Colt smiled at their little team joke. "Yeah we did." He sobered, though, as the door that Brenna had gone through opened. The nurse who walked out didn't approach them, instead went to the triage desk. "I only had one chance to get to Brenna. When I heard the ambulance he'd stolen had only recently had GPS installed I took a chance Nazer wouldn't know about it." He shrugged, grateful that information had fallen in his lap. It had led him straight to her. "Give yourself some credit, though. You thought of the earpiece so you guys could hear what was going on."

"I was worried when you were patted down, but Nazer was too busy moving up the timetable." Jake tilted his head and grinned. "Best case scenario." His eyes wandered to the double doors that Colt was riveted on. "Well, except for Brenna," he amended.

That was a pretty big exception, but Colt knew Jake hadn't forgotten what this had cost her. "Yeah." The feelings of camaraderie disappeared and the somber mood settled over them once more. It was hard to feel happy about anything when he didn't know what Brenna was facing.

Jake grimaced and shifted in his chair. "I'm sorry, man. You know what I meant."

"I know." Colt could tell he wished he could take back what he'd said, but he was right. Everything had worked out except for her being shot.

"How are your own wounds? Do you need to see the doctor?" Jake changed the subject, but Colt didn't want to talk about himself.

"Sore. But I've had worse. I'll just have Elliott look at it when we know Brenna's taken care of." He sat forward, his elbows on his knees. That was the most comfortable position right now anyway. "I've been meaning to ask you a personal question." He paused, trying to form the words without prying. "How do you and Mya make it work? Is it hard being a part of a task force together?"

Jake shook his head. "No. It's brought us closer because we both feel a part of something bigger than ourselves. Bringing down terrorist plots is a rush, as you well know."

Sometimes it was. Sitting in a hospital waiting room didn't feel so great. "Yeah, but don't you worry about Mya? Or does she worry about you?" Seeing Brenna in danger was something he wouldn't forget anytime soon.

"We trust each other to be careful, but yeah, that worry's

always there." Jake matched his position in the chair. "Brenna and Mya are headstrong women and they have a lot to offer Griffin Force. I know you see that. We'd be doing a disservice to the team if they stepped down so we wouldn't worry about them."

"No, I'd never do that. But what happened to Brenna today is going to haunt me." He flexed his fingers. Every protective instinct he had wanted to prevent a repeat of the events over the last few days from happening to her ever again. "I'll just have to find a way to deal with the concerns I have. Being with her is worth it."

Jake glanced up at the movement from the direction they'd come in. "Didn't you say you had a past with her? From the academy?"

"Yeah, we were close back then—" He started, but was cut off when a nurse approached them, a serious look on her face. His gut tightened and his mind went through all the scenarios he could think of. Was she . . . ? *No, she's still alive.* He had to believe that. "And if she'll have me, I'm going to have a future with her, too."

CHAPTER TWENTY

Brenna could hear voices. She wanted to open her eyes to see who was talking, but it felt like twenty-pound lead weights were on her face. Working harder to make her body respond, she opened them and blinked. She was in a hospital, that much was easy to see. Colt was sleeping in a chair next to her. Licking her lips, she tried to call out his name, but it was hardly more than a croak. That small noise woke him up, though.

"Bren?" He stood and leaned over her bed. "You're awake."

"Hey." She looked up into his familiar brown eyes and couldn't help the smile that spread across her face. "You look terrible."

He chuckled and pressed a soft kiss to her forehead. "You look beautiful."

"What happened?" Bits and pieces were coming back to her, but the full picture seemed hazy. "Did we stop Nazer?"

"There were some explosions, but not many casualties

beyond the bombers themselves." He gently took her hand, his thumb running lazy circles over it.

"What about the dirty bomb?" Her throat was so dry. "Tell me that didn't go off."

He shook his head, his grip on her hand tightening slightly. "Nope. All taken care of. And the British government is going to be cracking down on the disposal of hospital materials that could be used like that."

She closed her eyes for a moment. All good news, but she needed to know one more thing. "What about my brother? Is he safe?"

Colt sat down on the edge of the bed, putting their interlaced hands on his knee. "John's on his way back to Canada. He wants you to call him the second you can."

John was safe. The bomb hadn't gone off. That's what she'd wanted. She relaxed into her pillow, warmth shooting up her arm as Colt's fingers caressed her hand. It was a struggle to think of much beyond that. "Can I have a drink of water?"

"We really should call a nurse about that." He stood anyway, and poured her a cup of water from the pitcher on the table. Bringing it to her, he gently lifted her head so she could drink it. It was sort of a déjà vu from that day in the shack, only this time he was the one helping her get water. When she was done, he set the glass next to the pitcher and moved his chair closer to the bed. He sat down and picked up her hand again.

Brenna was starting to feel more herself, but she could tell he wasn't. He'd always been the adventurous one. Well, adventure-with-a-plan, at least. "Is everything okay? Since when are you a stickler for calling to check with nurses over water?"

She didn't think it was possible, but his expression turned

even more solemn, the light in his eyes dimming until she couldn't see it anymore. "Since you got shot," he murmured.

Her fingers tightened on his. That didn't sound positive. Was it worse than she thought? "How am I? Am I going to be okay?"

He leaned close, letting his other hand rest on the top of her head. "You were lucky. The bullet hit your spleen, which caused all the bleeding, but missed your intestine. So, you are now a woman without a spleen, but other than that, you should be good as new." He glanced behind them. "We should probably tell someone you're awake."

She let out the breath she'd been holding. *I'm okay.* "Do you mind if we don't call them just yet? I want to hear what happened." And have him all to herself a little while longer.

He gave her a half-grin as if he knew what she was thinking, but he humored her. "The British are calling us heroes. They've been really grateful for our help."

"The British love us? Well, that's a nice bonus then." She put her free hand down on the bed and changed position so she was on her good side, facing him. "So, it's over. We stopped the attack and captured Nazer." Relief coursed through her. Months of work and it had all turned out. All their gambles had paid off.

For the first time since she'd woken up, Colt took his eyes off of her and turned his face away. "Well, not quite."

"What do you mean?" A little sliver of doubt stabbed her gut. "What happened?"

She pulled on his hand and he turned back, his eyes full of guilt. "Nazer got away."

"What?" She moved to sit up, but searing pain at the movement forced her back. She definitely hadn't expected those three words to come out of his mouth. "How?"

"There was a miscommunication and he got away. Nate got a line on him, but so far, we haven't taken him in." He shook his head and ran a hand through his hair. "I should have stayed back to make sure he was secure."

"But you stayed with me." She sank back. "And now he's gone."

"No, no, don't even go there." He stood and tilted her chin to look at him. "It's not your fault. It's not anyone's fault. We got him once, we'll get him again."

Brenna met his gaze. She saw conviction there and she wanted to believe him. They both knew Nazer would go underground now and resurface when they least expected it. But Colt was right. They could find him again and they would.

"Did you question Cornell? With his trafficking connections, he could be Nazer's way out of the country." She wanted to sit up, grab a notepad, and talk through options. It was amazing how easily the pain went away when there was analysis to be made and work to be done.

"First thing. He seemed anxious to talk now that he's been connected to a terrorist and is facing some pretty serious charges to go along with that." Colt seemed to sense her intensity levels going up and he put his other hand on her arm. "It's all being taken care of. You just need to rest right now."

There was a knock at the door and Julian poked his head in. "Are you up for another visitor?"

"Of course." She rolled onto her back and pressed the button to sit her up slightly. It was obvious with the placement of her wound that changing positions was going to be difficult for a while. Her body definitely wasn't keeping up with what her mind wanted to do. "Can you put another pillow under my head?"

Colt grabbed an extra pillow and did as she asked. While he was arranging it behind her, Julian leaned against the wall. "I've got some good news. We've called in every favor we're owed and Mya tracked Nazer to France. He's become the top priority in pretty much every country in the world right now."

"Now that he's been compromised he's going to want a place to hide. So what's the strategy for grabbing him before he goes underground?" Brenna pinned Julian with her gaze. She would know if he wasn't telling her the whole truth.

Julian chuckled. "Don't worry about anything except healing right now. I've got everything under control and I'm heading to France as soon as I leave here."

"You can tell me," she grumbled. "I might be able to help."

Julian came to the foot of her bed. "You've gone above and beyond. I'm just happy to see you stuck around."

She looked between the two men. "Well, before you go, I have to know one thing. Why in the world did you let Colt come in alone?"

Julian gave Colt the side-eye and laughed. "Colt is one of the most organized people I know, but he threw that op together so fast it made my head spin and it was just crazy enough to work." He leaned against the footboard. "Colt found the stolen ambulance and you, faked his way in and made sure we could hear everything through his earpiece. But we didn't have enough time to figure out a way to get you out without setting anything off. And we needed to know where that bomb was going. So we kept our distance, but were following you both the entire time."

"So many things are making sense now." She smiled up at Colt. "Brilliant plan, really, but you could have given me a heads up. I thought we were facing that alone."

"I did, too, for a while," Colt said. "When I couldn't see even a hint we were being followed, I started to wonder if the earpiece was working. But it was." He squeezed her fingers. "They got to us about a minute after you passed out."

Brenna felt a flush creep up her neck remembering the seconds before she'd passed out. Her request for a kiss had resulted in a moment she'd never forget. "I kept wondering what the plan really was because it didn't look like it was work-ing. I've never been so scared in my life."

"Me, too." He took her hand in both of his and carefully lifted it to his heart. It was beating as fast as hers was. They had a lot to talk about the next time they were alone.

She tore her eyes away from Colt's and turned back to Julian. "So you were tracking us the whole time?"

"The team started to move in as soon as that guy mentioned PJHQ." Julian shifted and straightened. "I don't think I've ever been so panicked to hear an explosion and gunshots and not have eyes on the situation. I thought I'd lost both of you."

She shuddered, recalling how terrified she'd been herself right in the middle of it. "For a second I thought Colt had been shot, but then my side was hurting so bad. It took a minute to register it was me with the gunshot wound, but all I could think of was that I had to keep hold of that detonator, no matter what."

Colt kissed the back of her hand. "You did great. The team

picked us up and Elliott got you here in one piece." His eyes softened, the confidence she'd always seen there wavering a bit. "It was touch and go for a while, you know."

But she'd made it. They both had. "I'm sorry." She couldn't think of anything else to say that would ease his mind.

Julian interrupted. "I'm glad you're okay, Brenna. When you're released and have recovered, I'd like the two of you to come and see me in my office."

His tone was so serious it made Brenna think he was going to fire them. "Are you going to ask us to resign?" She didn't want to wait if that was the case. She had to know what he wanted to talk to them about right now.

"Why would I let the heroes of London resign?" He smiled and gave her a nod. "It's nothing like that. Come see me when you're ready for work again."

Brenna watched him go, the door quietly whooshing shut behind him. "What do you think that was all about?"

"I don't know. Maybe he has another assignment for us, but you need to take care of yourself first." Colt sat back down in his chair and picked up her hand again. "I think we need to talk."

"Me, too." Her mind went to the picture of his face above her, his lips on hers right before she lost consciousness. "I know you were trying to use our history to make Nazer believe you'd come in alone for me. So you don't have to worry about explaining any of that."

He looked at her for a long moment, then brought their entwined hands to his cheek. "Brenna, I meant every word."

She bit her lip, trying to hold back a smile. Elation rushed over her and the heartbeat monitor gave her racing heart away. "Are you sure?"

"I've never been more sure of anything." He reached out to cradle her face with his free hand. "It's always been you."

He moved closer, his eyes never leaving hers. She licked her lips, knowing that what happened now would change what she'd always thought she wanted. And all she wanted was this man in her life.

When his mouth finally touched hers, she closed her eyes, giving herself up to the moment. His lips were bold and teasing, just like him, but at the same time there was a quiet tenderness as he gently let his thumbs glide along her jawbone. Her skin tingled with awareness and she carefully lifted her hands to thread them through his hair. There was nothing held back as she returned his kiss. She wanted to show him how much she loved him and always would.

When they broke apart, he rested his forehead on hers. "I never should have let you walk away from me. I should have tried harder to show you we can make it work."

"Show me now." She tilted her head, her eyebrows raised in challenge.

He gave her the crooked grin that she loved. "Well, you know, we've really been working together on Griffin Force for months. And it's worked."

"That's a good point. So you're saying it works if we don't know we're working together?" She couldn't resist the happiness bubbling up inside her. "That's an interesting proposition."

"We make a good team and we've proven that now. I bet Julian would give us assignments that kept us on the same continents." He kissed her temple. "As soon as you're better of course."

"I bet he would, too." She was distracted as he kissed his way down her jaw.

"We have a lot of time to make up for," he said between kisses.

She finally pulled him back to her mouth. "I'm not going anywhere for a while, but we could get started." She caressed his stubbled cheeks and her thumbs trailed over his jawline. The monitors beeped crazily as her heart sped up. "Try to keep up with me will you?"

"Gladly," he said before his lips met hers again.

EPILOGUE

C olt opened the heavy glass door for Brenna, looking
up at the five-story office building. He'd never been
in Julian's "office" since he'd only ever had dealings
with him while they were in the field. "Have you been here
before?"

"Once." Brenna was dressed in a navy blue business suit.
She'd left her hair down, though, and it cascaded in waves to
her shoulders. She looked beautiful. And healthy.

He couldn't help but worry a little, though. "Are you feeling
okay?"

Her smile quickly turned to a scowl and she put a hand on
her hip. "What did I say about asking me that?"

"I know, I know, you're fine." Colt held up his hands in
mock surrender. "Don't give me that look. I'll do better."

She sniffed. "Do I have to remind you the doctor said everything looks good? I just have to take it easy for the next little
while. No lifting, stuff like that. I can walk to Julian's office."

She turned and pointed a finger at him. "And if Julian assigns us to help track Nazer in France, I'm well enough to take it. Just so we're clear."

"Yes, ma'am. I wouldn't say no to our very first assignment officially working together." He closed the gap between them and gave her a quick kiss.

She smiled up at him and his heart did a slow roll. Their relationship had blossomed quickly and while they hadn't picked up exactly where they'd left off, it had come pretty close. They'd added onto the foundation they'd built and from where Colt was standing, the future was looking pretty bright.

His hand slid down her arm and he cupped her elbow, staying close to her side as they walked to the receptionists' desk. The woman glanced up at them from her computer screen. "Can I help you?"

"We have an appointment with Mr. Bennet," Brenna said. "For Mr. Mitchell and Ms. Wilson."

The receptionist smiled. "Yes. He's waiting for you." She gestured toward the elevators. "He's on the top floor."

"Thank you," Brenna murmured, as she started in that direction. "It's a far cry from his office in Afghanistan, wouldn't you say?" she said to Colt over her shoulder.

Colt looked around at the glass tables and ultra-modern furnishings. Not a metal chair in sight. "Pretty much the opposite of what he called an office."

He watched Brenna walk a few steps in front of him. It seemed like a miracle. Her quick recovery had surprised everyone, even the doctors. But not him. She was a fighter and they had something worth fighting for.

At that moment, she turned around and reached a hand back for him. "You coming?"

He strode to her side. Gone were the days of watching her walk away. He took her hand in his and pressed a kiss to the back of it. "I'm right here."

Just where he wanted to be.

Don't miss the next book in the Griffin Force series, **The Capture.**

A daring rescue. A need for vengeance. Everything is on the line.

Julian Bennet, head of Griffin Force, finally finds love with Zaya Altes, but the day he buys her an engagement ring, international terrorist Nazer al-Raimi abducts her. Getting her back consumes him, yet it takes nearly a six months to find her. The daring mission to extract her from a hidden prison in Afghanistan is successful, but Zaya has suffered during captivity. Though she's grateful to Julian for breaking her out, she wants nothing to do with him. Before he can show her how much he still loves her, Nazer finds them and vows revenge. Can Julian keep Zaya safe and still stop Nazer once and for all?

Julie Coulter Bellon is an award-winning author of nearly two dozen published books. Her book All Fall Down won the RONE award for Best Suspense, Pocket Full of Posies won a RONE Honorable Mention for Best Suspense and The Captain was a RONE award finalist for Best Suspense. Most recently her books, The Capture and Second Look were both Whitney finalists for Best Suspense/Mystery.

Julie loves to travel and her favorite cities she's visited so far are probably Athens, Paris, Ottawa, and London. In her free time, she loves to read, write, teach, watch Hawaii Five-O, and eat Canadian chocolate. Not necessarily in that order.

If you'd like to be the first to hear about Julie's new projects and receive a free book, you can sign up to be part of her VIP group on her website www.juliebellon.com

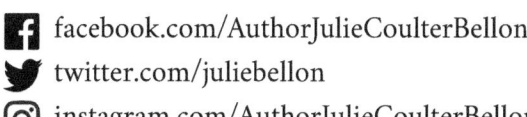

facebook.com/AuthorJulieCoulterBellon
twitter.com/juliebellon
instagram.com/AuthorJulieCoulterBellon